THOSE RUYS

on Planet Earth

To Mr. Seelig~
for a good laugh!

THOSE ROYS
on Planet Earth

By Robin Russell

Those Roys on Planet Earth by Robin Russell
Summary: Alex Roy and her sisters face the trials and
tribulations of an unconventional childhood.

ISBN: 978-1511606233
ISBN: 1511606231

Printed in USA
First Edition

For the best Arvonian mother a girl could have.
I miss you.

ACKNOWLEDGEMENTS

This book has been 15 years in the making and I'm grateful for the help of so many along the way.

To the early readers—Mom, Grandma Marge, Rima and Diem—I haven't forgotten your feedback, which included an ashen-faced "T.M.I." from Diem and more than one instance of "Has your sister read this?" from the rest.

To the middle constructionists—Ngoc and Stephanie—for their help maneuvering the initial diatribes into quirkier snippets.

To the cake-icers—Casey (no, not that Casey), Jill, Fifty, Heidi, Adrienne, Mario and Zoë (yes, that Zoë)—for assuring me the book was strange in all the right ways.

To the Jones-VanZandt-Andrade-Russell-Pan-Family Players—Margaret, Giovanna, Zoë (yes, again) and Rachel—for bringing my favorite excerpts to life.

To my editor, Cat McCarrey, for her candid "Gah!" and Greenlake walks. To my fellow Indie Author, Martina Dalton, for the gorgeous cover and help with the minutia. To Dennis VanZandt, whose talent for noticing mistakes rivals that of Aunt Harriet, the queen of flaw-disclosures.

I'm even grateful to my token curmudgeon friend, Alan, whose feedback kept me humble by consisting solely of, "It was funny, but easy to put down."

The Evidence

Setting the Stage
1

Mom's Postcard about Needing a Nap
An Introduction
Arvon
A Nuptial Account
Sample 1969 Marriage Announcement
Fictitious 1969 Marriage Announcement
The Golden Age *(AKA Bare-bottom)*

The Beginning of the End
13

A Recording
The Pain & the Great One *(AKA My Manifesto)*
Dad's Letter about Having Another Baby
(as if one wasn't bad enough)
Where Babies Come From
Alex's Diary Entry about Vulvas
Alex's Letter about Getting Ready for the Babby
Aunt Hattie's Letter about Capitalization & Not
Being an Insect

Three's Crowdeder
25

Of Aunts & Antics
45

The Family Dog
67

Cloaks & Daggers
81

Now Is the Summer of Our Discontent 109

Christmastime Is Fruit & Wine
151

The Voice
185

Zoltron
211

THOSE ROYS

on Planet Earth

Setting the Stage

Mom & Dad: young and blissfully in love

Alex: young and blissfully loved

June 2, 1971

Dear GREAT Aunt Hattie,

Hope this reaches you before Alex gets too old. She was born an hour ago via natural childbirth and with Walt in the delivery room. Esther says she looks like Walt. I'll wait until she's 12 before I say. That's all for now. Walt says I need some rest. Do I?

Love,

JR

An Introduction

My name is Alex Roy and I'm a girl. I know what you're thinking—that "Alex" is short for "Alexandra" or "Alexandria" or "Alexis" or some perfectly lovely name like that. It's not. It's just plain Alex. My parents wanted to protect me and my sisters from job discrimination so they gave us each gender-neutral names. They are forward-thinking people—pioneers in parenting—always planning for our futures.

My full name is Alex Justice Roy. This was my mother's doing. She used each of us as her own personal billboards. When we were little—before we knew better—she'd dress us in tee shirts which proclaimed: *A woman without a man is like a fish without a bicycle,* or *Join the army—travel to exotic lands, meet interesting people and kill them.* Her personal favorite was: *Ladies Sewing Circle and Terrorist Society.*

It could have been worse. My mother is a very opinionated woman and her ideas are certainly not limited to the realm of politics. My sisters are Casey Recycle Roy and Sam Floss Roy. We call her Sammy. One day, when I complained about my weirdo-name, my mother showed me my baby book. Inside was a piece of scrap paper with a list of possible names. Justice was clearly the preferred option. To give you a sense of how awful the others were, my second choice would have been "Return Library Books on Time."

By the way, while she was showing me my baby book, I noticed she'd crossed out "Fashions of the Time" and replaced it with "Movements of the Time." Underneath this revised heading she wrote:

The Women's Liberation Movement
The Gay Liberation Movement
The Bowel Movement

What will soon follow is a series of excerpts from our lives. Some might call them stories. I think of them more as evidence. That way, when my sisters and I grow up to be crazed lunatics or mass murderers, society will look back and see where it all went wrong. Of course with my sister's luck, we'll all end up with a bunch of Nobel prizes. I know this might seem like a good thing, but then the world will deify our mother's parental tactics and she'll become the next Dr. Spock. This is extra bizarre and funny because *she* personally has deified *Mister* Spock.

I say my sister's luck (Casey) because if anything bad is going to happen to anyone, it will happen to her. One summer, when she was hanging out with a *very* large group of friends, a dog made his way through the crowd to pee on one specific leg: hers. She was wearing shorts at the time.

Remember, if you find any amusement in this account, it's merely circumstantial. *This* is an exposé.

A. Roy

Arvon

Arvon is my mother's planet. She doesn't live there and she wasn't born there. But she's *from* there. At least that's what she told us when we were little. I think it is more her planet of convenience.

When we were growing up, it was her excuse for everything. If my sisters and I complained about washing the dishes or cleaning our rooms, my mother would remind us of the trials faced by children on her home planet.

"On Arvon kids don't even have dishes," she'd say as she motioned to a stack of dirty plates. "We all had to eat off the floor." Or "Be grateful you even have rooms. On Arvon we had to sleep in the mines."

My mother is a Star Trek fanatic. As children we weren't allowed to watch any television, except for Star Trek, which was mandatory. I thought it was the news.

"Why don't they ever tell stories about Arvon?" I asked, desiring some additional (and hopefully more objective) information. Even my mother couldn't know *everything* about her home planet.

"You want Arvon stories?" she demanded. "*I'll* give you Arvon stories."

My science teacher had never heard of Arvon.

"There's no such planet, hon," she soothed. "Maybe your mom just made it up to be funny."

Arvon was anything but funny. It was the strongest guiding force in our home—a force to be taken very seriously.

I waited months for the nerve to broach the subject with my mother.

"Yes, Alex. Your teacher was right," she began. "There are nine planets...in *this* solar system."

"*This* solar system," I confirmed.

"Right. Your teacher may not know about *all* the planets in the *entire* multi-verse."

"And that's where Arvon is?"

"Exactly," she said with a nod. "And Alex?"

"Yeah, Mom?"

"Remember." She hunkered down to look me directly in the eye. "Teachers don't know everything."

A Nuptial Account

In August of 1969, my unmarried parents sat in a German café, having just completed a backpacking trip across Europe. Earlier in the summer, in the most romantic city in the world,* my father had asked my mother to marry him. She had politely declined.

"Let's go to India instead," she had suggested brightly.

They sent the classic-Mom postcard to her parents on the way to the airport:

Mother and Dad—

   Gone to India. Don't wait up.

   Walt and Jillian

Standing in the Frankfurt Airport, my mother had a change of heart. "On second thought, I think I *would* like to marry you."

They returned to Seattle a few days after the postcard had arrived so my grandmother (who is an Olympic-level worrier) only had to lose a few nights of sleep. My mother was 18, the age of consent. For men, consenting age was 21, so my

---

* Detroit. Just kidding. It was Topeka. Hah! Got you again. It was— Fine, have it your way. It was *Paris*. Geesh, get a sense of humor, why don't you. We're only on page six after all.

dad needed to ask his mommy's permission to get married.

"You might as well," said Grandma Esther and they were married a week later.*

---

* By the way, this is a footnote. If you haven't already figured it out yet, it means I have some additional information that pertains to the material, but isn't significant enough to warrant being included directly. You might think of it as playing the role of the chorus in a Greek tragedy. Notice I didn't say "comedy." Anyway, there's no additional information here. It should be pretty self explanatory— assuming you have at least half a brain in your head.

Sample 1969 Marriage Announcement

John Moneybags and Lucy Mayflower

John Rapscallion Moneybags Jr. and Lucy Scatterbrain Mayflower pledged their marriage vows this afternoon at Saint Augustine's Lutheran Church in Greenwich, Connecticut.

The bridegroom is the pride and joy of former-senator John Rapscallion Moneybags Sr., President of Backroom Deals Incorporated, and Mrs. John Rapscallion✢ of Dover, Massachusetts.

This evening, the newlyweds will be honored with a reception at the Fancypants Country Club.

The bridal couple will make their home in Newport, Rhode Island, where Mr. Moneybags works as a nepotistic solicitor with the firm Ne'er-do-well and Sleezebucket.

There were 200 self-aggrandized guests at the wedding, including many high-muckety-mucks and snobs of every sort.

The bride wore an ivory Louis Vitton gown with Camelot sleeves. The cost of the wedding is estimated at $70,000.

✢ who apparently hasn't done anything remarkable.

Fictitious 1969 Marriage Announcement

My parents didn't have a wedding announcement printed up in the local paper, so here's my rendition:

Walter Roy and Jillian Johnson

Walter James Roy and Jillian Sue Johnson pledged their love this afternoon in the minister's study at Pilgrim Congregational Church in Seattle.

The bridegroom is a son of Esther Roy, nurse and single-mother. The bride is a daughter of Mabel Johnson, bookkeeper and professional worrier, and Roy Johnson, self-made man and graduate of the School of Hard Knocks.

This evening, the newlyweds will return to their campsite on Mount Baker, where they have been staying for some time.

There were five guests at the wedding, including two dogs of indeterminate breed. The bride wore a yellow mini-dress she made herself. The groom wore a tie he'd purchased from Goodwill. Short on funds, the couple used a purple, satin ribbon for a ring and hitchhiked to the wedding. Including the $10 paid to the minister, the cost of the wedding is estimated at $17.

The Golden Age

My parents lived in that campground for the first few months of their marriage. At first-frost, Grandma Mabel lured them home with pot roast. They stayed for dessert and a year.

My birth, which came a respectable two years later, launched what I came to regard, upon later reflection, as The Golden Age.❖ I was the first of my generation, with loads of aunts, uncles and grandparents who had nothing better to do than dote and coo and make me the focus of all attention. Whether traipsing with my parents across Europe, accompanying them to their college classes or snuggling in front of a fire, I had Mom and Dad all to myself. It was a two-to-one ratio and I was the one.

As with so many natural disasters, I didn't foresee the arrival of my new baby sister until it was too late. In the aftermath, it was still a two-to-one ratio, but I was no longer part of the equation.

❖ Since I was two when Casey was born, I can only imagine those days must have been my most content. In fact, it would have been absolutely idyllic if it weren't for one thing. I don't know what the deal was with my parents and half-naked babies, but *every* single picture from my years as a toddler has me wearing a hat, a tank-top or sweater (presumably depending on the season) and nothing else. Not "nothing" as in underwear or a diaper. "Nothing" as in N-O-T-H-I-N-G. To this day, my Uncle Ralph calls me, "Bare-bottom."

The Beginning of the End

Alex: age 6

Casey: age 4

Sammy: percolating

Mom & Dad: young

Aunt Hattie: old

A RECORDING

A Play in One Act

by

Alex Roy

TIME: Christmas, 1977

SETTING: We are in the living
             room of the ROY home.
             Stockings hang on the
             mantle above a crackling
             fire. There is a tape-
             recorder on the coffee
             table in front of a
             couch. It's a real
             Norman-Rockwell-Moment.✣

✣ Norman Rockwell (or as Casey calls him, *Ab-Normal* Rockwell) painted pictures about "everyday" American life. The only problem was that Americans weren't living like that *any* days, let alone *every* day. In the end, it just gave people a case of nostalgia over a life everyone thought everyone *else* was living. As a side note, even though he isn't considered by Art People as an "impressionist" *per se*, Casey says, "Oh, he gave people impressions alright—impressions of Planet Not!" And in this instance, I must agree with her.

Note: Just to be clear, Casey isn't saying this business about Ab-Normal Rockwell now. *Now*, she's four (as you'll soon see for yourself) and has yet to form strong opinions about art.

```
AT RISE:    WALT ROY, a young
            handsome father, is
            sitting on the couch.
            Beside him are his two
            daughters, ALEX ROY and
            CASEY ROY.
```

                    ALEX
        (cheerfully and dramatically
        singing into the recorder)
—in a one horse o-pen sleigh!

                    WALT
Beautiful, Alex. Now Casey, why
don't you sing your ABCs?

                    ALEX
        (obsequiously)
I can sing them, Daddy!

                    WALT
        (smiling genuinely at ALEX)
I know you can, Alex. Let Casey—

                    CASEY
        (interrupting and screaming
        into recorder)
I'm FO-WA!

                    WALT
        (softly soothing)
You sure are, Casey. You're four.
Can you sing your ABCs?

                    CASEY
        (hopping up and down)
I'm Foooo-waaaaaa!

                    ALEX
        (starting to sing quietly)
A...B...C...D—

                    WALT
        (lovingly but showing a
        modicum of irritation)
Alex, let Casey do it.

                    CASEY
Am I pretty, Daddy?

                    WALT
        (sighing)
Yes, Casey — very pretty.

                    ALEX
Daddy, if you want I can sing Once
a Lady Sailed Away.

                    WALT
        (resignedly)
Okay, Alex.

                    ALEX
        (loudly and with feeling)
Once a lady sailed away—

                    CASEY
Am I pretty, Daddy?

                    ALEX
          (singing more loudly)
—on a pleasant summer day—

                    WALT
          (sighing audibly)
Yes, Casey — very pretty.
          (calling off stage)
Jillian!

                    ALEX
          (practically screeching)
—on the back of a crocodile!

                    JILLIAN
          (off stage)
I'm making dinner.
          (adding calmly)
By the way, I'm pregnant.

                    WALT
          (with a look of panic on his
          face, he drops his head in
          his hands and groans)
Oh dear.

                    CASEY
          (bellowing before running
          pell-mell off stage)
I'M FOOOOOWAAAAAA!

                 (BLACKOUT)

The Pain and the Great One*
by Alex Roy

My sister's the pain,
And guess who's the great one.
She always complains,
And guess who's the great one.
About cars, trucks and trains,
And guess who's the great one.
About servants and maids,
And guess who's the great one.
She has a brain like a rock!
And guess who's the great one.
And thinks she's so hot!
And guess who's the great one.
My sister's the pain,
And I am the great one!

---

* I can only assume the title of the poem was inspired by Judy Blume's *The Pain and the Great One*, a picture book illustrated by Irene Trivas and published in 1974. I'm not sure how many zillion times I actually *read* it, but I do know I slept with it every night.

Dear Aunt Hattie, ❖

I hope this letter finds you well. Things are always lively here, what with the girls and all. Speaking of whom, Jillian and I thought having a third might settle the other two down a bit. Jillian is pregnant and we are all very excited, more or less. I hope you'll be able to visit us again this summer. It's always a delight to have you around and I know the girls enjoy your company tremendously. Keep well and keep us apprised of any future travel plans.

Much love and God bless,

Walt

❖ If you can't read cursive, basically this is a letter my dad wrote to Aunt Hattie telling her that he and my mom were going to have yet *another* baby. You'd think they would have learned their lesson with the last one. I think he is trying to be funny. Trust me, if it *was* funny, I would have put it into non-cursive for you. It's not and you should feel free to go to the next page without any fear of judgment from me. Although, you have to admit that not being able to read cursive *is* kind of stupid.

Where Babies Come From*

Alex: Mom?

Jillian *(reading either the newspaper or some kind of how-to guide—this detail is fuzzy. The point is, she keeps reading it throughout the conversation, even when it's her turn to talk)*: Yes.**

Alex: Where do babies come from?

Jillian: Blah blah...ovary...blah blah...Fallopian...blah blah...vulva...blah blah...testes...blah blah...cervix...blah blah...contraction...blah blah...epidural...blah blah...and next thing you know, you've got another one.

Alex: Oh.

Jillian: Anything else you want to know?

Alex: Uh...no.

Jillian: Good. Glad I could help.

---

* This is my best recollection, which might be a tad faulty. I was six after all.

** Not "Yes?" as in, "Yes, dear child, what need dost thou have of me?" but "Yes," as in "Yes, I am your mother."

Dear Diary,

Well, Mom and Dad are going to have ANOTHER baby. I hope it's a good one this time.

I asked Mom where babies came from and now I'm more confused than before.

I told my friend Nate and he said that his mom has a vulva too. It's blue and she drives him to school in it every day.

Sincerely,

A. Roy

Dear Ant Hattie,

Thank you for the Books and clothes. We are getting ready for The babby. Happy New Year! I am doing very good work in School.

Sincerely,

Alex

Dear Alex,

Firstly, it's "Aunt" Hattie. I am not an insect. Secondly, neither "school" nor "books" are proper nouns, nor do they commence a sentence. Therefore, neither requires capitalization, of which you seem exceptionally fond. Thirdly, I believe you meant "baby" since there is no such thing as a "babby."

Finally, while I'm pleased that you are doing "very good work in school," I'm quite dismayed at the quality of education you are receiving, especially as it pertains to grammar. I shall speak to your father about this.

Aunt Hattie

Three's Crowdeder

Alex: age 7

Casey: age 5

Sammy: age 1

Mom & Dad: young but tired

Aunt Hattie: really old

An Encounter

Scene opens and a five-year-old Casey is in the process of strangling Rufus, the neighbor's dog, by using his leash to tie him to the highest rung of the staircase.

Alex (*entering from Stage Left):* Casey! (*rushes to untie Rufus) W*hat are you doing?

Casey (*hands on hips*): He wouldn't do what I told him to do.

(Rufus is now dry-heaving.)

Alex: Well, what'd you tell him to do?

Casey: I told him not to be a dog.

Acorns for Alfred
by Alex Roy

On a very cool day in Kansas, in the deep woods, there was a huge oak and in that tree was a family of squirrels. The mother's name was Catherine. The father's name was Charlie. They had three children. The oldest was Betty. The smallest was Jeff.

They were a very happy family except for one thing. Their middle son was so bad. He was always that way. Once he brought a rat into the home. And he WAS curious!

"Alfred," his mother called.

"What?" said Alfred.

"Will you do me an errand?"

"No," said Alfred.

He was bad.

"I'll do you the errand, Mother," said Betty.

"Okay, Betty. Go get me some acorns."

Betty worked very hard and got a lot of acorns but Alfred ate them all.

Dear Diary,

Tomorrow in church, Casey, Sammy and I are getting baptized! I was going to ask Mom to explain it to me but when she explains stuff, I always get more confused.

Instead, I asked my dad! He said getting baptized means God loves me very much and will forever and ever.

Then I asked him why Casey was getting baptized and he sent me to my room. From now on, if I want to know something, I'm just going to ask Ant Hattie.

Sincerely,

A. Roy

P.S. I know I put Ant Hattie instead of Aunt Hattie. I put it as a joke!

P.P.S. Ha ha ha!

An Accusation

(Alex enters the house, wobbling. She has a faint ring around her mouth approximately the size of a gas tank opening.)

Jillian: What were you doing?

Alex: I could tell you, but you're not going to like the answer.

Jillian: Let me smell your breath.

(Alex holds her breath and shakes her head vigorously.)

Jillian: You've been huffing gasoline again.✣

Alex *(trying to speak without exhaling):* I like the smell.

Jillian *(muttering to herself):* One would think I'd have given birth to smarter children.

✣ *Occasionally*, when I was bored, I'd climb onto my dad's motorcycle and pretend I was in an all-girl biker gang called *The Pinkies*. My favorite thing was to remove the gas cap and smell inside until my mother would yell, "Get your nose out of there!" Again, this was not a regular occurrence, despite Casey's *alleged* evidence to the contrary.

The Great Idea

When Sammy was a baby, she wouldn't sleep unless she was holding my mom's finger. She didn't just cry without it, she wailed. Because only Mom's finger would work, it didn't really bother the rest of us and we were all free to move about our daily lives. It bothered my mother a lot. She was the kind of woman who would get antsy if there was more than one person ahead of her in the grocery line. Sometimes, it seemed as if she were trying to live three lives in one.

So my mother (who is nothing if not ingenious) came up with what she called a "great idea." From an old box of Halloween costumes, she found a fake witch's finger and put it on. Once Sammy fell asleep, my mother slipped her finger out and snuck downstairs to get some work done while her weirdo baby slept peacefully.

As with many of my mother's ideas, this one was only half-baked. And if we thought Sammy cried loudly before, it was nothing compared to the fire-engine-siren howls emanating from her bedroom when she awoke to find—not only had her mother vanished—but somehow, she was also dismembered.

From that moment on, we would all cringe any time my mother would say, "I've got a great idea!"

B is for Bedtime Stories

My father told wonderful bedtime stories. Each night, it was the same comforting ritual.

"What'll it be tonight, girls?" he'd commence the routine.

In unison, we'd shout, "Princesses!"

"Then princesses it is!" He'd dim the lights, settle into his chair and ask in mock absentmindedness, "Now, how does it start?"

"Once upon a time, Daddy," I'd prompt, eager to play my part in the charade.

"Oh yes, once upon a time. I see." Clearing his throat he'd begin. "Once upon a time, there lived a brave and intelligent princess."

"And beautiful," Casey would interrupt.

"Hmm?"

"She has to be beautiful!" we'd insist. This was non-negotiable in any and all stories.

In the early days, my father (ever the feminist) would try to convince us that a princess did not have to be beautiful and that bravery and smarts were infinitely more valuable. Those days went the way of *The Barbie Ban*. Now, misogynistic carcasses littered our bedroom floor and pink, frilly dresses clogged our closets. The moral fiber of my father's stories had been compromised.

"Of course, Casey," my father would sigh heavily. "The princess was intelligent and brave and beautiful."

Settings would vary, names would change, but the plot was wonderfully predictable. Night after night, we would happily receive the generic tale of Cinderella-Snow White-Sleeping Beauty.

Then my father got a job singing at a dinner theater.

"Who will tuck us in?" I asked.

Wariness spread from me to include Casey. "You won't tuck us in?" Casey's indifference turned sour.

"I'll be working, honey." He hugged her tightly. "Your mother will tuck you in."

Casey and I exchanged a furtive and fretful glance. This was not good.

The night of my father's first performance came a month later.

After putting Sammy in her crib, my mother asked, "Do you *goils*✢ want a story?"

A cloud of apprehension and dread settled over us and, after an awkward silence, I murmured, "Sure."

"Very well," my mother said as she began tucking us in, with none of the care and panache my father showed.

When it came to bed-tucking, my father was like a butler with ambiguously magical powers— sort of a younger brother of Mary Poppins. My mother, on the other hand, *poked* rather than

---

✢ "*Goils*" was the term my mother had coined when speaking to us *en masse*.

tucked, and showed all the care of a prison warden.

I went on the offensive and blurted, "Mom, could it not be about Arvon?"*

She seemed slightly annoyed at my audacity but considered my request.

"Fine. How about the Oregon Trail?" It was one of those questions that *wasn't* a question.

Interpreting our silence as acceptance, she turned off the lights, sat down and began her history lecture. Within minutes, the story had turned from Manifest Destiny to food shortages, broken wagons, deadly illnesses and the bitter cold. Then it went from bad to worse.

The first bedtime story my mother ever told us was of The Donner Party.**

The next night, our minds still flooded with images of familial cannibalism (my mother had gone into great and academic detail), she told one of Aesop's lesser-known fables—the one about Isadora Duncan, a great dancer, who died a horrible death when her scarf (a symbol of her

---

* I knew better than to request a princess story outright. Where my father would occasionally relent, set aside the parenting agenda and indulge us, my mother's position was clear and unflinching. Every interaction she had with us had a purpose, an intended outcome. There was no room for fancy.

** A group of pioneers who got stuck in the snow and ate each other. Why they called it a "party" is beyond me. Casey thinks it's because it was the birthday of one of the pioneers. Some birthday.

vanity according to my mother) caught in the wheel of her car and strangled her.

Over the course of my father's short career as an entertainer, my mother must have told us hundreds of stories. I remember each and every one of them. Many were of the Holocaust, including a large sub-section devoted entirely to the "experiments" of Dr. Mengele.

Once, she told us about the Elephant Man, a severely deformed and shunned man from Olden Times whose desperation forced him to earn money by letting people pay to see his disfigurements. We were sad instead of terrified that night.

By the time my father had finished *My Fair Lady* and *South Pacific*, we were a pitiful combination of bloodshot eyes, frayed nerves and the jitters.

"You tell her. You're older," Casey pleaded one evening.

The sun was setting. We didn't have much time.

"Fine," I snapped. "But you have to help."

She agreed and that night we synchronized our attack. Together we rallied every last whine, plea and tantrum. Finally, my mother agreed to tell us a normal story.

"How about a princess story?" she asked in a cloying voice.

Casey nodded excitedly and climbed into bed. Truth be told, I did the same. We weren't the smartest children in the world, but even so, we should have known better.

"Once upon a time," my mother began (and it seemed too good to be true), "there lived a beautiful princess named Arianna who wanted nothing more than to marry a handsome prince."

So far, so good.

"In a neighboring kingdom there happened to live a handsome prince and when he heard of Arianna's beauty, he asked his parents to send for her. When she arrived at the castle, Arianna and the prince fell instantly and totally in love. After a far-too-short courtship, they decided to wed.

"Upon hearing of her son's intent to marry Arianna, the Queen reminded the prince of their kingdom's tradition. He could choose any princess he fancied, as long as she could fit into the 'royal shoes.'"

This was different.

Perhaps if we had been more awake or less naïve, we might have sooner realized this story was not quite what it seemed. My mother, being an exceptionally tall woman and having exceptionally large feet herself, had a *thing* about feet. Most would call it an obsession, but compared to hailing from a planet no one knew existed, the foot thing was just a thing.

The story went on.

"The next day, over breakfast, the prince presented the 'royal shoes' to his betrothed. Arianna looked closely at the shoes as her fiancée explained the custom. Arianna noticed the shoes were dwarfishly small. She knew they would never fit her normal-size feet."

The sudden plot twist looped in my brain. Now, I was fully awake.

My mother, warming to the tale, continued almost rabidly. "The prince handed Arianna the shoes. She took them and tried to place one on her foot." *Pause for effect.* "It didn't fit."

Now, even Casey seemed suspicious.

It was too late to stop her. Mom was on a roll.

"Arianna and the prince were devastated. After all, he was handsome and she was beautiful. They *belonged* together. They *had* to get married. Arianna moped all day long. At night, she lay in her bed, tossing and turning, unable to sleep. Then, just before the sun was about to rise, Arianna had a 'great idea.'* Quietly, so as not to disturb anyone in the castle, Arianna slipped out of bed and sneaked out of her room."

Now, I was confused. The story was actually getting good. It had a plot and everything. My mother *had* to be up to something.

"Arianna tiptoed through the halls and down the stairs until she came to the castle's kitchen."

We were completely alert and sitting straight up in our beds. An impish smile crept over my mother's face and my stomach turned.

"There on the counter, Arianna saw the solution to all her problems."

---

* I believe I've already covered what my mother considered a "great idea."

Here it comes.

"A butcher knife!"

"Oh no!" I yelled, indignantly.

"Mom!" Casey protested.

She ignored us, racing toward the story's crescendo. "Arianna placed her foot on the butcher block, raised the knife and...HACK! HACK!" Mom motioned wildly with her arm. "HACK! HACK!" she cried again. "The beautiful Arianna chopped three inches off her left foot."

"Mom, please," we begged.

"Howling in pain, Arianna forced herself to lower her left foot, which was now gushing blood. Next she raised her right foot onto the counter and—"

"Mom, no!" we shouted again.

"HACK! HACK!"

We screamed and Sammy began crying in the next room.

"She cut off three inches from her *right* foot! But Arianna was strong and didn't faint, even though she was in more agony than she had ever known. Painstakingly, she crawled back up the steps and down the hall, dragging her bloody, mangled feet behind her."

My mother rose from her chair. She retrieved Sammy and held her gently. I can remember it vividly—her silhouette in the doorway, Sammy cooing serenely in her arms, my heart racing and a look of sheer horror covering Casey's face.

"Wh...wh...what happened to Arianna?" she stammered.

My mother stroked Sammy's hair and returned her to the crib. I was dumbfounded. Not from the story. It was mild next to her ghastly history lessons. I simply couldn't reconcile the juxtaposition I was witnessing. Holding Sammy, she seemed compassionate, knowing how (and wanting) to comfort her child.

I knew my mother was not a cruel woman. I think she honestly didn't know she had been terrorizing us night after night. She thought she was teaching us. She was trying to show us that justice was more important than vanity; that dignity and survival win over pettiness and sexism. She thought she was expanding our worldview. She thought we were getting a kick out of it. I'm almost certain she didn't mean us any harm.

"She fit into the shoes, Casey," my mother answered absentmindedly.

"Didn't that hurt?"

"I imagine it was quite excruciating."

I listened to the sounds of her putting my sleeping sister back to bed.

"Good night, *goils*."

"Mom?" I called.

"Hmm?"

"Did it turn out okay?" I was hesitant. "I mean, did they live happily ever after?"

"Of course. They just needed to build some ramps in the castle. Now good night and get some sleep." She began to close the door.

"Ramps for what?" Casey asked from underneath her covers.

"For Arianna's wheelchair."

"Oh," we said, our voices flat.

"Goodnight, *goils*."

"Goodnight, Mom."

Lexicon of My Mother

Referring to us as "*goils*" was just the tip of the iceberg. If you were going to understand anything my mother said you were going to have to learn her language, which (like everything else she did) was a moving target.

That being said, it will behoove you to at least familiarize yourself with some of it.

Channeling her inner 1930s Chicago gangster, words like "girls" or "church" or pretty much anything with ir/ur sounds, were changed to oi/oy sounds. For example: *goils* and *choych*.

My mother also didn't subscribe to what she referred to as "the silent letter nonsense." Therefore, knife was "ka-nife" and scissors were "ski-sors" and so forth.

And while she had by no stretch of the imagination mastered any second language, that didn't stop her from being open to as many different languages as possible. And since they say you have to "use it or lose it," my mother systematically replaced words in English with the new words she learned. For example, salt and pepper were *salz und pfeffer* not occasionally, but forever. In fact, it wasn't until I was at a friend's house and asked for the *salz und pfeffer* that I found out these words weren't even English after all.

Fly Thighs Boom Boom

My mother composed two songs. The first she wrote when I was seven and we were on a very long car trip through rural Canada. Whenever we saw a cow, which as you can probably surmise was quite frequently considering we were in rural Canada, my mother would break out in song.

"Hi Cowie Wowie! Boom! Boom!"

It may seem short but with incessant repetition it can really rack up the minutes.

Her second song was composed on a train going west.

"Oh, I went to a restaurant to get something to eat and the waiter asked me what I wanted and I said...FLY THIGHS! Boom! Boom! FLY THIGHS! Boom! Boom! The bees are so jealous! The bees are so jealous of...FLY THIGHS! Boom! Boom! Yes, FLY THIGHS! Boom! Boom!"❖

❖ She never did compose a third song, but I think we can all agree that if she had, it would have inevitably included a rousing chorus of boom-booms.

Interview with My Hero (Jillian Roy)
by Alex Roy

My hero's name is My Mom. She also goes by Jillian Roy. I hope you enjoy my interview with Jillian Roy! Here it is!

Question: What's your name?

Answer: Jillian Roy.

Question: What is your favorite animal?

Answer: Chicken.

Question: What is your favorite song?

Answer: Bob Dylan's Subterranean Homesick Blues.

Question: What would you do if you could do anything over?

Answer: Wait to have children.

An Interview-ish

Casey *(enters kitchen holding a yellow notepad and marker with the cap still on)*: Alex, what's your name?

Alex: Go away.

Casey: *(whining)* I want to interview *you*.

Alex: *(sighs)* Fine. My name is Miss Shut-up-and-leave-me-alone.

Casey *(pretends to write and mumbles a repetition of the name)*: ...leave...me...alone. What's your favorite animal?

Alex: Your face.

Casey *(smiles proudly and pretends to write)*: ...my...face. What's your favorite song?

Alex: The sound of you leaving.

Casey: What would *you* do if you could do anything over?

Alex: Not agree to this interview.

Of Aunts
& Antics

Alex: age 8

Casey: age 6

Sammy: age 2

Mom & Dad: youngish

Aunt Hattie: really, really old

Maiden Aunts

My father only had Maiden Aunts and Aunt Hattie was the cream of the crop. She was just over five feet tall and utterly tactless. She wore matching polyester pantsuits in every shade of yellow known to man. In glaring contrast, she had strawberry-blonde hair courtesy of Clairol's Nice 'n Easy shade 127. Aunt Hattie was a powerhouse.

She was also the healthiest person I knew. She never got colds or flus, *and* she had regular and solid bowel movements (or at least that's what she told us regularly and solidly). In fact, in spite of smoking constantly, eating three gallons of ice cream per week and drinking more than her fair share of Stingers,* she was the picture of health.

She is not the rarity in our family. Men may not live that long, but the women last forever. Whether they never marry or outlive three husbands, whether they eat fried everything or a slab of bologna for dinner, whether they are vigorous and rowdy or dainty and reserved, the women in my family last.

---

* I'm not sure about the exact recipe, but from the one time I sneaked a sip, it tasted like one part mouthwash to two parts gasoline. As you may recall, I knew all about gasoline.

The Goldsmobile

Aunt Hattie drove a 1973 gold, gas-guzzling Oldsmobile Cutlass Supreme, which we, understandably and affectionately, called "The Goldsmobile." By sitting on three pillows, Aunt Hattie was able to see over the steering wheel, but it was a lot of bother for nothing because the car was so filled with cigarette smoke it didn't make much of a difference. Aunt Hattie thought opening the windows would muss up her hair.

There were two reasons she never got in a car accident while driving in town. First, it was a small town and everyone knew enough to clear out of her way. Second, she never drove more than 15 miles per hour. In fact, we could ride our bikes faster—although we only tried racing her once.

Every winter, Aunt Hattie would migrate from Maine to Florida, often with a cat in the passenger seat. I have no idea why she didn't get into any accidents doing this, especially considering she never drove *less* than 80 miles per hour and talked to truckers on her CB radio the entire way.

One final note about The Goldsmobile. The color was officially Mayan Gold. Now, I don't know if the hair came first and the car came second or if it was the other way around. All I do know is that Oldsmobile's Mayan Gold is the exact color of Clairol's Nice 'n Easy shade 127.

Christmas Presents

Aunt Hattie spent her summers shopping for our Christmas presents. Bit by bit, each day, she'd drive around in The Goldsmobile to frequent rummage sales. By the end of the summer, she would've accumulated an odd assortment of gifts for each of us. Aunt Hattie was a generous person.

One year, we received the following:

For my father: a package of way-too-big underwear, a deck of Delta Airlines playing cards and some deodorant. *Did I mention she was tactless?*

For my mother: a hospital gown, some bizarre exercise contraption with ropes and pulleys *circa* 1940 and an exceedingly garish polyester scarf.❖

For me: two boxes of stationery (one with dolphins that I knew she got for free from the World Wildlife Fund, and the other an assortment of Get Well Soon cards), the "G" volume of a 1954 children's encyclopedia and a sweater that would fit Casey, but which neither of us would be caught dead in.

For Casey: one box of stationery with purple and lime-green flowers, and the most jacked-up

---

❖ Aunt Hattie made no secret of the fact that she thought my mother's coloring as well as her wardrobe were too drab. Once she told me, "I can barely tell your mother is there. It feels like she's sneaking up on me." I think the colorful piece of clothing was Aunt Hattie's version of a cow bell.

Barbie Doll any of us had ever seen.* Casey promptly threw both gifts in the garbage.** Her last present was a lemon-yellow tee shirt with blue lettering that read: Misunderstood. She wore it for a month straight.

For Sammy: a game of *Candy Land* (with half of the pieces missing), a Hot Wheels car (which Sammy liked to chew on since she was two years old and still teething) and some World Wildlife Fund stickers, which Casey promptly stole.

---

* *Sigh.* I don't even know where to begin on this one. I guess I'll just take it from head to toe. Barbie's hair was shaved on the sides, short on top and long in the back. I believe it's called a "mullet." Her shirt had the sleeves cut off and she was wearing a pair of Ken's pants. Someone had inked tattoos on her arm, including one that read, "Madge" and there were thick, black slashes along her calves, making it look like she had hairy legs of Mediterranean proportions. The feet were the worst. They had been cut off at the ankle and taped back on, so that, if positioned carefully, Barbie could literally stand on her own two feet instead of needing high-heels or a man—or even a wall for that matter. My mom took one look at the monstrosity and said, "Nicely done, Aunt Hattie. This is a doll I can work with."

** Later, when Casey wasn't looking, I retrieved the stationery. And because I was a good sister, I never used it when I wrote to Aunt Hattie because I knew she'd then know Casey had thrown her gift away. In the end, it was kind of pointless since I didn't write to anyone except Aunt Hattie anyway. Still, when it comes down to fishing presents out of the trash, it's the thought that counts.

Dear Aunt Hattie,

How are you? I am fine. Thank you for the stationary and for the "G" encyclopedia. Do you know what gargoyles are? I do now! I also know about glands and gladiators. I hope you will visit us soon!

Sincerely,
Alex

P.S. Why are they called gladiators? I was reading about the things they did. Ouch! They should have been called SADiators! Ha ha ha!

P.P.S. Or MADiators! Ha ha ha ha!

Dear Alex,

Stationary is a synonym for motionless. Your present, while certainly not mobile, was nonetheless not stationary, but stationery.

Regarding gladiators, the name has very little to do with their emotional state. Rather, the word stems from the Latin "gladius" meaning "sword." As such, gladiator is synonymous with "swordsman."

As dismaying as your spelling may be, I certainly appreciate your inquisitive mind. I am happy to answer your questions via the post, as a personal visit is highly unlikely.

Aunt Hattie

Cooking

Aunt Hattie hated to cook and found some very creative ways to avoid it. One would think, since she loathed preparing food, she would be very grateful to those who prepared it for her. Not Aunt Hattie. She was very good at criticizing everything and everyone.

Aunt Hattie *(waddling into the kitchen with a Stinger in one hand and a Pall Mall* in the other):* What's for dinner?

Jillian: Spaghetti.

Aunt Hattie *(with a look of undisguised disappointment):* Paster? *(That's Maine for "pasta.")* Oh, for crying out loud. I'm so sick of paster.

Jillian: You're welcome to make something else.

Aunt Hattie *(resignedly)*: Paster's fine.

---

* Pall Malls are cigarettes specifically engineered for old people. There's something in the atomic composition that makes the ash stay on despite being waved about in conversational gesticulations.

Aunt Hattie Chores

Aunt Hattie ran a tight ship and she held people to their promises. Whenever we would visit, we weren't let in the door without signing up for one of the myriad tasks on her list. As children, our jobs were small—squash aluminum cans—hang wash on line—return smutty romance novels to library.[❖] My father got the harder stuff—fix leaky faucet—put car up on blocks for the winter—mow the acre of lawn. In all of my memories, I can't think of a single time Aunt Hattie asked my mother to do anything.

"Why doesn't Mom ever have to work?" I asked one day as Aunt Hattie loaded me up with wet sheets, clothespins and old-lady bras.

She paused to take a drag off the cigarette hanging precariously from her lower lip. "Because your mother does things in a *different* way."

"You mean an *Arvon* way?" I asked in a hushed voice.

"Precisely."

❖ This was Casey's favorite job. I have to admit, it was impressive how quickly she could read an entire book and still be walking at the same time.

The Whipping Incident

Once upon a time, Casey and I nearly drove my mother crazy. We were ramped up on sugar from candy we'd purchased with change stolen from Dad's dresser. We were fighting. We would not listen to her. We were in rare form.

"Just go up to your room!" she screamed in exasperation.

We froze. She never yelled. As the two of us trudged upstairs, I saw Mom sit down at the dining room table and put her head in her hands. I felt horrible.

At that time, we were obsessed with the world of *Little House on the Prairie*.✣ That's where I got the idea. I went into my parents' room and opened up their closet. I took one of my father's belts off its hook and walked stoically down the stairs. My mother was still at the table.

"Here, Ma," I said softly, in my best country accent. I was holding out the belt. It was a beautiful scene—the heroine ascending to an even higher level of piety, offering herself for sacrifice, taking on the sins of all mankind. "Ya cin whup may if'n ya wanna," I drawled with my chin held high so as to give the imaginary cameras my best angle.

She did.

✣ A series of books by *Laura Ingalls Wilder* about her life growing up in a little house on the prairie in Olden Times. We would frequently call our parents "Ma" and "Pa" as a result.

She got a good whack in too, before I jumped out of her reach.

"Mom!" I shouted, dumbstruck. I couldn't believe she would actually do it.

"What?" she said, already looking more relaxed.

"You hit me!"

I couldn't believe it. This was not in the script. She was supposed to throw down the belt, pull me into an embrace and announce that I was the best daughter—miles above Casey in her eyes. She was *supposed* to say it was all a test to see which of her daughters had the moral fortitude to face the brutalities life had to offer.

But my mother is the inventor of plot twists.

"You offered," she said matter-of-factly.

I started to sniffle, and rub my thigh where a red welt was beginning to form. "But...but...you weren't *supposed* to."

My mother set the belt on the table and looked me straight in the eye. "Alex," she said pointedly. "If you don't want someone to hurt you, don't ask them to."

Dear Aunt Hattie, *

It's a rainy afternoon here in Seattle—surprise, surprise. My mother took the girls to Farrell's for ice cream sundaes, which means Jillian and I have a few hours of quiet. Right now, she is using the time to alphabetize the spices. I'm not quite sure why, but she certainly seems to be enjoying herself. For me, I wanted to write you since it's been too long.

Tomorrow, I'll be singing a solo in church—Thou Shalt Bring Them In. It's part of Handel's Oratorio, Israel in Egypt. Thinking about Moses leading his people through the desert is helpful, especially when I begin to tally up my own struggles, which certainly pale in comparison. Jillian will be the liturgist and

---

* The only thing interesting in this letter is that Dad asks Aunt Hattie if she wants to visit, which I'll tell you now, she most certainly does not. I think she's afraid we'll give her a heart attack, which is probably right. The rest of the letter is a bunch of boring church stuff.

Alex and/or Casey will be the acolytes, depending on how well they are getting along in the morning. I suppose, if little Sammy could take the offering, it would be a whole-family affair.

Jillian and I want to know if you'd like to spend part of the summer with us. We have a room all ready for you. I hope you are doing well. How is your health?

Much love and God bless,
Walt

Dear Walter,

I am doing reasonably well, considering the fact that I've recently forayed into the realm of the octogenarians.* I imagine things are quite lively around your house. I wouldn't be surprised if even Moses himself would prefer the desert.

Life here is quiet and picturesque. Although I'm sure spending time with you and your family would provide some interesting anecdotes to share with my friends, I must admit my reluctance. After all, I'm quite old and your girls are not.

Aunt Hattie

---

* This is Aunt Hattie's hoity-toity way of saying she's 80 now.

Tights

When it comes down to it, "Preparation" was the only game we really played. The titles were different—*Princesses, Underroos, Bear Town, Olden Times*, *School*—but the actual game itself was comprised almost entirely of the elaborate staging. There were costumes to make and scenery to design.* Most importantly, we needed to develop a believable back story. What were the religious traditions in Bear Town? What bank and postal systems needed to be established so Olden Times was more realistic? What kind of school was it and which subjects were taught?

We spent most of our time and imagination on social infrastructure. We'd spend hours rearranging the house for *1850's Gold Rush* and only play for half an hour before getting in a fight over authenticity and the rights of women to own land. In a series of huffs and mutterings, we'd go our separate ways and only reconvene later to argue over who was going to clean up.

No matter the game, long hair was unequivocally required. Casey and I coveted the

---

* This was probably the easiest part. Costumes were curtains nearly every time. Not curtains from the linen closet or some old box in the basement. We used the curtains already in place, since (obviously) we needed the curtain rods as well. They made perfect wands or walking sticks, depending on the game. The scenery inevitably just meant rearranging the furniture throughout the house.

flowing tresses of other girls. Even a girl with hair touching her shoulders was the object of our envy. In fact, that's probably why Casey and I have such good posture to this day. We were always trying to stand as tall as we could, so our hair wouldn't touch our shoulders. Because once it did, the gig was up and my mother would haul us off to the barber shop. Yes, the *barber shop*—not a salon, where a hairdresser could have at least styled it. We were smacked down in front of an old man with a crew cut who gave my mom a three-for-one special. ❖

But ingenuity must be hereditary, because Casey and I found a way around this. First, we compensated by wearing the girliest dresses we could. This annoyed my mother to no end, especially when Casey "forgot" to wear underwear or somehow lost it mid-day. Second, we found a substitute for hair: tights. We'd each stretch a pair of tights (green, purple, white—it mattered not) over our head and pretend we had two ponytails cascading down to our knees. We soon discovered that if one was good, three were better.

❖ Sammy never seemed to mind having short hair and she happily wore jeans and a tee-shirt. In fact, both she and my mother were regularly mistaken for father and son, which amused Casey and me tremendously.

"And what's your little brother's name?" some benevolent stranger would ask.

"Sam," we'd answer sweetly.

It always seemed strange that we never got in trouble for this.

The only problem was, the tights were true to their name. They were actually quite *tight*. So after playing all weekend, wearing our flowing tresses non-stop (yes, even sleeping), we'd have deep grooves in our foreheads, which would last well into the week.

Obviously, on top of the tights we'd wear underwear. After all, they made perfect hats. They fit our heads and conveniently had two perfectly proportionate holes for our colorful locks.

The Kidnapper

Even more fun than having long hair, was playing with the frame of Sammy's baby buggy. Casey and I would take turns squeezing into it and parading each other up and down our block. One day, I was pushing Casey when a man appeared on the corner.

"I'll give you a dime if you show me where the park is down the street," he said, pointing in the opposite direction of the park.

"We're not allowed to cross the street without an adult," I said meekly.

"I'm an adult," he reasoned. "I'm sure it'll be alright."

"I'll do it!" Casey piped up, starting to get out of the buggy.

I shoved her back in. "No you won't," I said sternly. "We have to go."

"You can't tell me what to do," she sassed back, climbing out of the buggy and walking toward the man.

"Casey, get back here!" I snapped. "We need to go home!"

"She'll be fine," the man said as he reached for her hand.

I grabbed a hollering and struggling Casey, crammed her back in the buggy and raced home. Mom was in the driveway, getting into the car.

"Mom!" I screamed, my voice carrying over the din Casey was making in the buggy. I told her what happened as I gasped for breath.

Great in any emergency, my mother took immediate action. "Walt, call the police. Girls, get in the house."

That's when I knew it was serious. Not that Dad was calling the police, but that she didn't call us "*goils*." Strange as it may seem, *that* was what scared me.

The police came and a lady cop asked me a lot of questions. It made me feel important and brave and mature. In fact, I would have been the center of attention if Casey hadn't been running throughout the house shrieking, "Kidnapper! Kidnapper! Kidnapper!" like a maniac.

Dear Jesus,

Forgive me for wishing sometimes that the kidnapper had taken Casey. I hope you know it is only on the very hard days.

Sincerely,

A. Roy

Dear Walter,

Upon further consideration and learning of recent events, I have decided to visit you this summer after all. Frankly, with the way things are being run over there, I might not have any grand nieces left before too long. I've booked a flight for the first of June. Please have the following ready for me upon my arrival:

1. Stinger
2. Ashtray
3. Shuffled deck of cards in reasonably good condition.
4. Cribbage board
5. Three grand nieces, also in reasonably good condition.

Aunt Hattie

The Family Dog

Alex: age 9

Casey: age 7

Sammy: age 21—you'll see

Mom & Dad: 75% old and 25% young

Aunt Hattie: 100% ancient

The Little Woman *

One Saturday, in the early days of my parents' marriage, my father had The Guys over for poker.

"Well, is that little woman of yours going to make us some sandwiches?" one of his friends asked.

"Jillian?" my father called.

No answer, so he got up and went to find her.

She was on the back porch visiting with the neighbor's dog. By the way, when I say "visiting," I mean *actually* visiting. She was having a for-real conversation. Not with the neighbor, who was nowhere near, but with the dog.

"Jillian," my father interrupted. "Will you make some sandwiches or something for The Guys?"

She looked at him quizzically, which probably included a dog-like tilt of the head. "Sure." **

About a half-hour later, my mother emerged from the kitchen. She was wearing an apron and had smeared flour over her face and arms. At first glance, one might have thought she'd been cooking for hours, especially with that big ceramic bowl she

---

* "The Little Woman" was a derogatory term for wife. It was right up there with "toots," which incidentally, my mother used all the time when she was talking to us individually. As in, "Get in the car, toots," or "Brush your teeth, toots."

** Although I wasn't there at the time, I'm absolutely certain this is where the camera would have zoomed in to show the mischievous gleam in her eye.

was carrying. She set the bowl in the center of the table with a dramatic gesture that translated as "*Voila!* Dinner is served."

It was filled with dog food.

Dear Diary,

At last, after waiting patiently for seven years, something good has happened to me. FINALLY Aunt Hattie left!!!! I feel like I can breathe again and not choke choke choke on all her nasty smoke smoke smoke. Plus, she's sooooooooooo mean!!!! She's positively diabolical!!!! But just when I thought we could be a normal family for ONCE in my life, I found Sammy eating the dog food someone left on a table!!!!

Sad again,

Casey

The New Dog

When Sammy was three-years-old, she insisted she was a dog. She would only answer if you barked to her and she would only eat if Mom put the food in a dog dish and set it next to the back door. She would sleep at the foot of my parents' bed, even though my father tried to insist that dogs should sleep on the floor. It seemed harmless enough at the time, so we humored her. Casey, however, became incensed and refused to communicate in Doggyese (as my mom referred to it). Day by day, she became growlier and growlier, which when you think about it, is actually kind of funny.

A Dispute

Casey *(stomping into the kitchen):* I've had enough of this garbage! Sammy is not a dog! *You* know she's not a dog. Daddy knows she's not a dog. Even Alex knows she's not a dog and Alex is as dumb as a rock. Why do Sammy and Alex get to do whatever they want and I don't? It's not fair!

(Casey puts her hands on her hips and begins tapping her foot as she waits impatiently for her mother's response.)

Casey *(with mounting irritation):* Well? Aren't you going to say anything?

Jillian: *Woof!*

Dear Aunt Hattie,

How are you? I am fine. Have you ever had a puppy? We do! Surprise! It's Sammy. She's the best puppy ever. She's lots of fun to play with although she does have a few bad habits. She likes to lick your face and bite Casey. What's a muzzle?

Goodbye! I love you! I hope you will come visit us again soon so you can see our puppy before she becomes a dog and isn't so cute.

Sincerely,
Alex

A One-Sided Conversation

Walt: (*answering telephone*): Good evening, Roy Residence—Aunt Hattie! It's so nice to—

Pause.

Walt: A dog? You don't say.

Long pause.

Walt: Well, that's certainly something to think about.

Very long pause.

Walt: Well, thank you for letting me know. Do you think you'll be able to make it out for a visit soon?

Short pause.

Walt: Oh yes, I see. Well, that certainly can—

Shorter pause.

Walt: Okay then. Take care, Aunt Hattie. Thanks for calling. We love you.

Forbidden Words

My parents were always very conscientious about the language we used. Although the mandates included speaking politely and using correct grammar, there were other rules as well. For example:

We couldn't say "gypped" because it was offensive to gypsies. Casey tried to point out that there weren't any gypsies around, but my mother said, "It doesn't work like that." Instead of "retarded" we said "obtuse" and we weren't permitted to say "starving" because it was offensive to people who were *actually* starving. Instead, we were "famished" or "ravenous." And despite Casey's sound argument, we couldn't say "just kidding" after using one of these "forbidden" words because apparently it didn't "work like that" either.

We couldn't say "conned" because Mom said it was related to "convict" and it undermined the principle that someone could pay their debt to society and be given a true second chance. I *tried* to explain to my mother that if someone goes to jail it is *because* they did something bad and we shouldn't trust them anymore.

She promptly responded, "Alex, I would remind you that this world is complex. There is more out there you *don't* understand than you *do*. Furthermore, I would remind you of some particular people who went to jail for—as you say—"doing something bad," including Gandhi, Martin Luther King and Our-Lord-Jesus-Christ. I can only assume you are not trying to say we shouldn't trust them."

"No, Ma."

"That's what I thought."

Funereal Rehearsals

My mother drilled us regularly. "Burial or cremation?"

"Cremation!" Casey and I would shout like game show contestants.

"Woof!" Sammy would echo.

"Excellent. You are good Arvonian children."

We'd glow.

"What else?" she'd continue.

"A big party," I'd say seriously.

"With ballet dancers," Casey would add while spinning around the room.

"Casey." My mom would put her hands on her hips and give her The Look.

"I want ballet dancers," she'd whine.

"This is *my* funeral we're talking about. At yours, you can have as many dancers as you want."

"Fine. I want a million."

"Great. I should be long gone by then. So what two songs do I want played at *my* funeral, Casey?"

Casey would warble, "And in the end..."

"Good, and Alex?"

"Bob Dylan's Dream."

Casey would switch songs mid-note and continue with renewed vigor. "While riding on a train goin' west, I fell asleep for to take my rest."

"That'll do, Casey."

"I dreeeeeeamed a dreeeeeeam that made me sad-d-d-d—"

"Go play, *goils*."

An Altercation

When Casey and I couldn't share, Mom would make us take a break from playing with the dog. As children who had an exorbitant amount of free and unsupervised time on their hands—like, A LOT—we had plenty of opportunities to let our imaginations run amok.

Alex: Casey, look! We can turn our bikes over and spin the wheels to pretend they're ice cream makers!

Casey *(snidely)*: Or we could just ride them, you retar—

Alex: Mom! Casey said—ouch! MOM! Casey pinched—OUCH!

Dear Aunt Hattie,

How are you? I am fine. Great news! Sammy doesn't have to be our dog anymore because we got a real one!

Mom named him Roy's Regret. Casey calls him Princess and Dad just calls him The Dog. Sammy calls him a name I can't really spell because it's pretty much just a bark.

Dr. Terasaki says that's because Sammy is in a period of acculturation and readjustment.

I try to call Roy's Regret by his real name as often as I can because I don't want him to get too confused. He seems easily confused but he was like that when we got him.

What will you call him when you visit us next? When will you visit us next? Excavating minds want to know! We all want it to be soon soon soon!

Sincerely,
Alex

P.S. Just so you know, Dr. Terasaki is a psychologist! I didn't want you to think he was a veterinarian. We sure know better than that! Ha ha ha!

Cloaks & Daggers

Alex: age 10

Casey: age 8

Sammy: age 4

Roy's Regret: no clue

Mom & Dad: 85% old and 15% young

Aunt Hattie: prehistoric

Dear Diary,

It is New Year's Day and I am determined to be faithful to you this year. I know I have never actually done this before but I promise this will be the year! I will write down everything that happens to me in exquisite detail so I can look back as an adult and be impressed with how advanced I was at my age.

I also promise I will obey my parents and not fight so much with Casey—even if she starts it. I'm older now and more mature. By the way, Casey, if you are reading this then you should know I found the note about Nick so if you breathe one word about my diary to anyone I'm going to tell him.

Also, I may or may not have spit on your toothbrush.

Sincerely,

A. Roy

Citizens of the World

We were always boycotting something. Every time I even *looked* at some candy bars, I felt guilty, imagining mothers being forced to give their babies formula mixed with contaminated water. Often, we simply went without. While one product had its parent company in apartheid-ruled South Africa, another product was manufactured in sweatshops or built weapons or bombed clinics.

Shopping with my mother took forever.

Once, we tried to trick her by hiding her *Shopping for a Better World Guide*, but she just sat patiently in the car lecturing us about global economics and corporate manipulation until Casey fished the book out of her underwear. Another time, I remember Mom standing in front of the spaghetti shelf for nearly twenty minutes as she debated between purchasing a brand whose parent company polluted the environment and one that used slave labor in China. That night we ate Marinara sauce over rice, which is apparently how they have it on Arvon anyway.

Even so, exposing us to the world's culinary delights was a high priority for my mother. She made food from Senegal, Poland and India. We ate shark, tongue and snails. She'd spend hours in the library perusing recipes from across the world. She'd special-order food from the local health food store, and was determined that in some way we would experience the diversity the world had to offer.

And when her recipes didn't quite work out, we were informed they were Arvonese.

"It's Arvonian Stew."

"It's Sauce d'Arvon."

"They're Arvon Cakes."

Sammy loved every single thing my mother ever cooked.

"Mom's such a great cook!" she would exclaim, causing Casey and me to look at each other in shared disbelief. "We are soooo lucky!"

This phenomenon of Sammy's enthusiasm only served to encourage Mom's culinary explorations. As for me and Casey, our favorite dinner, by far (and to my mother's extreme frustration), was my father's Tuna Fish and Noodles. A can of tuna fish, a can of Cream of Mushroom soup, and a package of egg noodles. Boil, drain, mix, serve.

Dear Diary,

Today I told Mom she wasn't my real mom because my real mom wears high heels and bakes cookies instead of a bunch of Arvon crap. But then Mom said, "Well, your real mom should come get you then."

I can't believe my own mother disowned me today! I'm only eight!

Miserable and motherless,

Casey

P.S. If Alex is reading this, she should know I don't care if she spit on my toothbrush, because I use hers anyway so ha ha ha!

Dear Diary,

Here is the status of my New Year's resolutions:

1. I haven't written down anything because nothing interesting has happened yet. I fear, dear diary, if this keeps up you will soon be rendered a notebook.
2. I have managed to obey my parents, although it's mostly because they haven't ordered me to do anything unreasonable yet.
3. I also haven't fought with Casey, although it has only been a week and I do have a sense that something is building.

Sincerely,
A. Roy

P.S. If you are reading this and your name is Casey, I put my toothbrush in the toilet, so it looks like the joke's on you!

P.P.S. If you are reading this and your name is not Casey, then—no offense—but you should mind your own business!

Third Grade Personal Narrative
by Casey Roy

Once upon a time, I was in the back seat of a taxi with my stupid sister Alex and my mean Aunt Hattie. Sometimes, Aunt Hattie is mean by accident and sometimes she is mean on purpose. Alex is always stupid on purpose. In this Personal Narrative, when we were in the taxi, Aunt Hattie is mean by accident. By the way, a Personal Narrative is a boring story about your life and can't be about fairies even if you know in your heart they are real. It also can't be about Planet Arvon, but that's fine because I get enough of that Arvon business at home.

So join me in the back seat of my Personal Narrative. Don't worry. There's plenty of room because you don't exist.

"Aunt Hattie, you are so smart," says Alex. "Someday, me hope me am as smart as you!"

"That's incorrect grammar, Alex," says Aunt Hattie. "You mean 'I' not 'me.' Someday, 'I' hope 'I' am as smart as you."

"That's not very smart, Aunt Hattie," I say, which isn't considered mean because it's true.

Here is where the mean-by-accident thing happens.

Aunt Hattie says, "I am so lucky to have two such wonderful grand nieces." She looks at me and says, "One who is so pretty," and looks at Alex to say, "and one who is so smart."

"Dang, Aunt Hattie," I say (except I didn't say 'dang,' I said the other word but

my teacher, Mr. McCullough, made me take it
out because my mother was going to see this
Personal Narrative and I said like heck she
was because as soon as I got this stupid
Personal Narrative back, I was going to
throw it in the garbage and then Mr.
McCullough asked me if I would like to go to
the principal's office and I said no and then
he said it wasn't a question and then I said
well, why did you ask it and then I had to
go to the principal's office anyway).

But all of that was later. Now, we're
still in the taxi and Aunt Hattie said what
she said, so I said what I said, which was,
"Dang, Aunt Hattie. You might as well call
us dumb and ugly."

Then, she got mad and told my father.
So in the end, because of MEAN Aunt
Hattie, I got sent to my room for swearing

AND to the principal's office for being honest about it. In other words, I was punished twice and called stupid.

The End

P.S. Thank the Lord! If I ever have to write another Personal Narrative, I'll go straight to the principal's office and pluck out my eyeballs.

P.P.S. It is true that I am the pretty one though.

Dear Aunt Hattie,

How are you? I am fine. Thank you for the birthday present! I'm not sure exactly what it is, but when I figure it out, I'll write you a nother thank you to be more specific.

I can't believe I'm already ten years old. Do you remember when you were ten? Casey wants to know if you rode a dinosaur to school, but I assume you didn't. I imagine Dinosaurs were pretty expensive and I know you don't like to spend money unless you absolutely have to. Dad calls you parsimonious. Mom has a nother word for it but I can't remember it right now.

Anyways, we love you and miss you tons. When are you coming to see us again? We all hope it is soon soon soon!

Sincerely,

Alex

Dear Alex,

Neither "nother" nor "anyways" are words. I believe you meant "another" and "anyway." Also, as I've mentioned before, your capitalization needs improvement, especially regarding proper nouns, which dinosaur is not.

Speaking of dinosaurs, you can tell your sister I did not ride a dinosaur to school because school was within walking distance. As to how I spent my time when I was your age, I believe I spent it trying to mind my own business. As you would say, ha ha ha.

I'm not sure when my next visit will be. I'm still recovering from the last one.

Aunt Hattie

Dear Aunt Hattie,

How are you? I am fine. Thank you for correcting my letter! I appreciate it. Casey says it'll be a cold day in you-know-where before she ever sends you another thank you note. I completely disagree. That's how we learn! Thank you for correcting me so much. You are perfect at it!

Sincerely,
Alex

P.S. Congratulations on trying to make a joke! I didn't understand why it was funny, but that just means you need to try harder next time, ha ha ha ha ha ha ha!

The French Game

When I could bribe or blackmail my sisters, my favorite game to play was *The French Game*. Casey and Sammy weren't as keen on it, since it revolved around me and they had to sit around for most of the time.

The game was simple. We'd begin the morning by building a solid back story. As you may recall, we were experts at this. We'd tell all the neighborhood kids (a dozen or so, assuming The-Boys-across-the-Street* were around) how excited we were that our cousin Petunia was to arrive that very day.

With a glare and a shove from me, the action would commence.

After sighing and rolling her eyes, Casey would say blandly, "She's from France."

"And pretty," Sammy would add, and hopefully not in her robot-zombie voice.

"Yes, that's true. She's exceptionally beautiful." I'd include a great deal of animation, trying to compensate for their lackluster performances.

"She's coming this afternoon," Casey would continue.

---

* Across the street lived a family with a whole mess of kids. The two outliers were girls and way too old or young to be of any use. The rest—maybe six or seven of them—were boys. It was perfect—with enough human girth for us to play all the good games. I'm sure they had individual names at the time, but we never knew them. They were simply and always, the-boys-across-the-street.

"And?" I'd prompt, with an elbow-jab if necessary.

"And I'm ever so excited."

"Will you look out for her?" I'd ask. "She hasn't been here in a while. Also, she's very beautiful and so might get abducted."

They would agree and the scene would be set. After lunch, I'd dress up in one of my mother's fancy business suits, find an empty suitcase, grab a map and leave out the back door. From there, I'd climb the fence and fight my way through three feet of blackberry brambles before emerging in the neighbor's backyard. I'd sneak across to the next block and walk around until I was at the beginning of ours.

Once I was sure my hair was free of twigs and I had wiped away most of the dirt and blood, I'd take out the map and begin walking toward our house, peering alternately at the map and various house numbers.

All the neighborhood kids would be hanging out on our porch and someone would yell out, "Alex! What are you doing?"

I'd ignore them and walk by the house.

"Alex!"

I'd turn and say softly (and in my best French accent), "*Eez* it *zat* you are talking *avec moi?*"

Gales of laughter.

"Alex, why are you talking like that?"

"Who is *zees* Alex? *Je suis* Petunia, from *Fronz*,"❖ I'd say indignantly. After all, you know how the French can be.

"Come on, Alex, we know it's you."

"Oh, I see. You must be *sinking* of my *coozeen Aleeex*. It is she whom I have come to see, all *zee* way from *Fronz*."

They would look a little less certain and this was Casey's cue.

She'd come running out of the house crying, "Petunia!" before hugging me in a vice-like grip and whispering, "I'm only going to do if for ten minutes and I want two Twix."

"Ah, Casey, it *eez* being so good to see you," I'd respond theatrically, as I gave her an equally hard hug and added, "You better do it good."

Then to the audience, I'd cry, "And where *eez Aleeex*? My beautiful *coozeen* said she would be here to me meet me—her *coozeen* Petunia, from *Fronz*."

"She was just here a second ago," Casey would say in wide-eyed, mock innocence. Now that she finally had something fun to do, she'd get into it.

❖ I don't know why, but it somehow seemed necessary to drop my voice an octave when I said "Fronz." Perhaps it made it sound even more foreign and exotic. Regardless, if you are somehow in a situation where you are reading this book aloud, make sure you include that part. If you aren't reading it aloud, you should do so at least for this one. Believe me, it's worth it. And if you are worried about people losing respect for you, don't bother. My mom explained that we think people have a lot more respect for us than they actually do.

Things would continue like this until everyone was convinced (we didn't live on the smartest block) and all of the kids were scouring the neighborhood for me. And, after milking this for as long as I dared, the real melodrama would kick in.

"Alas," I'd say, with the back of my hand on my forehead. "I must go. *Zee* plane *eez* leaving to take *zee beautiful* Petunia back to *Fronz* and I haven't even seen my sweet, beautiful, intelligent *couzeeen Aleeex*." With my performance complete, I'd exit block-left.

After turning the corner, I'd race down the hill, cross the neighbor's lawn and force my way back through the bushes. I'd hurl my suitcase and map across the fence, scale it and run breathless through the back door. A quick change of clothes and I was on the front porch—scratched, bleeding and breathless.

"Hey, what's up?" I'd ask casually.

It was the best game ever.

Dear GREAT Aunt Hattie,

Sammy still has the flu and I think she may have given it to Roy's Regret. He has been vomiting all morning. Either that or he was a victim in the latest antics of Alex and Casey. When they get along, they are as thick as thieves. Now they are fighting again and it feels like World War III. Walt is at a spiritual retreat with some other laypeople from church so Bob Dylan and I are holding down the fort. Don't you wish you were here?

Love,

JR

Dear Jillian,

It sounds like a mixture of a three ring circus, a convalescent home and a mental institution over there. Forgive me if I pass on the invitation.

Things are going well here. The NASDAQ* was up this week, which always helps my bowels. I tend to sleep better also. There was a fat, orange cat snooping around yesterday and I put out some canned food for her.

Life is peaceful and I have plenty of room. Perhaps you should leave some canned food out for the girls so you and Walter can visit me. As Alex would say, ha ha ha!

Aunt Hattie

---

* I have no idea what this NASDAQ business is, but I can tell you that when it's up, Aunt Hattie drinks three stingers and when it's down, she drinks four.

Dear Diary,

I just intercepted a message that proves Aunt Hattie is trying to kidnap my own parents from me! She is positively diabolical!!!!

In fear of abandonment,

Casey

P.S. In other news, I told Sammy I could digest furniture and she started crying and stamping her foot. It was so funny!

P.P.S. I'm still super sad though because Aunt Hattie is trying to tear apart my beloved family.

Kidnapping Revisited

Once, I asked Casey if she wanted to play *Kidnapper*.

"How do you play?" she asked suspiciously.

"Oh, it's lots of fun!" I said excitedly. "Just walk down the hallway and I'll jump out and kidnap you."

She hesitated for a minute before saying, "Okay." ✢

"Great! Just give me a few minutes. I'll let you know when."

Ten minutes later, Casey took those historic steps down the hallway.

"Aha!" I yelled, jumping out of the bedroom and covering her with a bedspread.

Casey screamed.

"*Goils!*" my mother called from downstairs.

Neither of us answered. I was focused on the task at hand and Casey was gagged by that point. Deftly, I dragged her body into her bedroom and began binding her with various belts and scarves.

"Mmmf!" Casey's grunt was surprisingly realistic.

"Alex!" This time is was Dad.

"Shhh," I told Casey, "or we'll get in trouble."

She was quiet.

"Yeah, Dad?" I called back casually.

✢ According to the lawyer, this is the part that was considered "consent."

"Dinner's almost ready. Come and set the table."

"Okay—I'll be down in a minute."

"Now," he yelled.

"Okay, coming," I called back, trying to think of what do to with Casey.

"Mmmf!"

I decided it was best to just lean her against the wall. "Okay, Case," I said. "I'm going to set the table, but I'll be back in just a sec. Okay?"

The bedspread shook its head emphatically.

"It'll just be a second," I said. "Then you can kidnap me."

The bedspread thought about it. "Mmf mmf."

"Great, I'll be right back—just don't move."

I was folding the napkins when it happened—all in slow motion: a massive crash from upstairs that reverberated throughout the house—my mom looking to the ceiling where the plaster was losing purchase—and my dad turning to look me dead in the eye.

It was the middle of winter and I didn't have shoes on. Nevertheless, I ran out of that house faster than I ever had before. I kept running until I was about a half-mile away. Hours later, when I had to choose between hypothermia and the consequences of my actions, I returned home.

Dear Mom and Dad,

I'm sorry I kidnapped Casey and broke her nose. I know I am being so much trouble. I am simply trying to make my way through.

I am really jealous of Casey and Sammy because they get so much attention. That's not an excuse. It's just a fact of my life these days.

Sorrily,
A. Roy

P.S. I will try extra hard not to kidnap Casey anymore.

P.P.S. If I do have to kidnap her, I will try extra, extra hard not to break her nose again.

Dear Walter,

There was a special program on Phil Donahue last week. It was called Teenagers: The Plague of America. Needless to say, I haven't been able to sleep since. The issues discussed were deeply disturbing and the "guests" were even more so. Such coarse language and bad grammar!

I am very concerned about Casey. It is imperative that she spend the summer with me. My neighbor (you remember Goldie) and I are planning what Phil calls an Intervention. I'm afraid I must insist.

If you like, you may also send Alex. I'm sure Goldie and I could use the help.

Enclosed is a check to cover the plane tickets. I'll deduct the money from your inheritance.

Aunt Hattie

Dear Aunt Hattie, *

Thank you for offering to host Alex and Casey this summer. We accept! The girls are very excited. They get out of school early on the seventh so Jillian booked a flight for that afternoon. The girls will be on opposite ends of the plane, which is probably best for them, not to mention their fellow passengers. Thank you again. I know you will have a splendid time together and make some beautiful memories. I'm enclosing some paperwork, in the likelihood that Casey tries to tell the authorities she doesn't know you.

Much love and God bless,
Walt

---

* This letter is a bunch of flowery butt-kissing that pretty much boils down to: "Gee, Aunt Hattie, thanks for taking our rotten kids off our hands before they drive us nuts!"

Dear GREAT Aunt Hattie,

I'm glad you've decided to take on the girls this summer. As the saying goes, what doesn't kill you makes you stronger! I advise you to keep their toothbrushes under lock and key, otherwise you'll never get them to brush their teeth.

Love,

JR

Dear Diary,

Nooooooo! I just found out Aunt Hattie is not kidnapping my parents. She is kidnapping me!!!! She's positively diabolical!!!! I told Mom and Dad I would not stand for it and they called me petulant!!!! Can you believe that??? I'm determined to fight this at all costs. If I have to, I will escape into the woods and move in with a pack of wolves. Even if they tear me limb from limb and I have to watch them eat my own body from my decapitated head lying in the dirt with ants crawling all over my eyeballs, it will be better than living with Aunt Hattie for even one minute!

Desperately,

Casey

P.S. At least I will get a break from stupid Alex. She is driving me crazy!!!!

Now Is the Summer of Our Discontent

Alex: age 11

Casey: age 9

Sammy: age 5

Roy's Regret: "no clue" plus a year

Mom & Dad: 95% old and 5% young

Aunt Hattie: *circa* Dawn of Time

Dear Mom, Dad, Sammy & Roy's Regret,

How are you? We are fine. The plane ride was great! Casey and I pretended we were orphans from Zanzibar and Casey got called "precocious," which Aunt Hattie says is different from "precious." Casey says she's both, but that's Casey for you! Ha ha ha!

Last night was our first night so Aunt Hattie didn't make us do any chores. Instead, we explored the attic while Aunt Hattie "relaxed" on the porch. Have you ever had a Stinger? I'm asking this to Mom and Dad, not Sammy and Roy's Regret. Anyway, if not, I think you wouldn't like them.

Guess what we had for dinner. Cereal! It was an adventure. Well, I had cereal. Aunt Hattie had some cigarettes and Casey just glared at us. You know the look. Do you remember on the third floor there are only two tiny rooms? Aunt Hattie calls one "the girls' room" and one "the boys' room." The Girls' Room is pink and full of dolls. The Boys' Room is brown and full of books! Can you believe that? It made me laugh and laugh. Then Casey and

I "argued" a little. Don't worry, Dad. We mostly used our words.

Anyway, both Casey and I tried to convince Aunt Hattie we were actually boys and had just been fooling her all along. She told us she didn't just fall off the turnip truck and to get our butts in bed.

Well, I should get some sleep. It'll probably be a big day tomorrow. Aunt Hattie keeps talking about what's in store for us. Casey thinks that means shopping but I'm not so sure. I think I'll dream about what my chores will be. Anyway, I love you and miss you!

Sincerely,

A. Roy

P.S. I got The Boys' Room! I have a gigantic bruise on my arm from you-know-whom. It hurts like the dickens but it was worth it!

Aunt Hattie's Schedule

Upon retirement from nursing, Aunt Hattie followed the same daily schedule with near-military precision:

7:00: Begin getting out of bed.

7:15: Finish getting out of bed.

7:20: Eat breakfast, which consisted of weak instant coffee and an English muffin with discount margarine, orange marmalade and a copy of *U.S. News & World Report.*

7:50: Smoke first Pall Mall of the day.

8:00: B.M❖

8:20: Wash❖❖ and dress.

8:30: Review stock portfolio, pay bills and take care of other related business.

9:00: Correspondence

9:30: Attempt crossword puzzle from the 1950s (she was solving them chronologically), smoke, sigh heavily and stare expectantly out the front parlor window.

❖ As a former nurse, Aunt Hattie always used the proper terms for anything related to bodily functions. B.M. stands for "Bowel Movement." Regular people just say poop. Actually, *regular* people probably don't update their family on their poopage at all.

❖❖ I say "wash" instead of "bathe" because to my recollection, I never saw or heard of Aunt Hattie cleaning herself with anything but a soapy washcloth in one hand and a Pall Mall in the other.

10:30: Flirt shamelessly with Ned, the mailman, which would make me laugh and Casey gag. After Ned left, Aunt Hattie would sort mail and sing *Tiptoe through the Tulips*. When she would get to the part about "kissing in the moonlit garden," Casey would burst into convulsions of disgust before running up to the third floor and covering her head with every pillow she could find.

11:30: Eat lunch* with *U.S. News & World Report.*

12:00: Work** in garden.

12:30: Rinse cereal bowl and dish out an entire pint of ice cream.

12:50: Unplug phone (so as not to be disturbed) and turn on television.

1:00: Watch *All My Children* and hook rugs.***

---

* Lunch for Aunt Hattie was always some kind of bran cereal. She didn't care which, as long as it was cheap. When she'd empty one box, she'd just reach for the next one, even if it meant eating expired food and mixing cereals like *Raisin Bran* and *Wheat Chex.* Ignored expiration dates were one of many things Casey hated about staying with Aunt Hattie. She said it was "positively diabolical."

** I use this term loosely. Basically, gardening to Aunt Hattie consisted of being in the garden and eavesdropping on the neighbors, with a hose in one hand and a you-know-what in the other. And if you don't know what I mean by a "you-know-what," then you really haven't been paying attention and probably should start reading easier books.

*** Aunt Hattie managed to make about one rug a year. She probably could have made more if she had used both hands.

2:00: Errand or Bridge Club

5:00: Nurse her Stinger on the lanai, which is a hoity-toity word for porch.

6:00: Eat dinner❖ with *U.S. News & World Report.*

7:00: Wash underwear in sink so she could put off having to do laundry as long as possible.

7:15: Get *on* bed instead of *in* it, so she wouldn't have to make it in the morning and so as to put off washing sheets for as long as possible.

7:30: Read smutty romance novels, smoke, eat ice cream and listen to conservative talk radio.

9:30: Grumble that Walter never called to check on her and make sure she was still alive.

10:00: Try to sleep.

10:30: Remember to plug the phone back in.

❖ One of Aunt Hattie's most frequent meals consisted of one piece of fried bologna with horseradish sauce, seven canned green beans, half a small baked potato and another pint of ice cream.

A BUTTING OF HEADS

_____

A Play in One Act

by

Alex Roy

TIME: Summer, 1982

SETTING: We are in the kitchen of
            AUNT HATTIE'S home.
            Clearly, it was once-
            impressive but now shows
            signs of wear. It's a
            less creepy version of
            Miss Havisham's mansion.

AT RISE: ALEX ROY is eating
            cereal in a breakfast
            nook while her sister,
            CASEY ROY, sulks across
            the table from her. AUNT
            HATTIE enters, smoking a
            Pall Mall and holding a
            mug with a bank logo on
            it. She's wearing horn-
            rimmed glasses, a lemon-
            yellow house coat and a
            wary expression.

                    AUNT HATTIE
              (cigarette in mouth)
Good morning, girls. I trust you
slept well. Be sure to make your
beds or you'll get a demerit.

                    CASEY
I don't know what a demerit is,
but I don't want one and I don't
want any of that stinkin' cereal.
              (She motions disgustedly to a
              box of Bran Flakes that
              looks about as old as the
              kitchen itself.)

                    ALEX
              (cheerfully)
I don't mind eating your stinking
cereal much at all, Aunt Hattie,
and I do know what a demerit is.

                    CASEY
              (muttering)
Do you know what a kiss-ass is?

              (ALEX kicks her under the
              table and CASEY flinches
              before giving a menacing
              glare in return.)

                    AUNT HATTIE
Well, Casey, you could have a
banana.

CASEY

I hate bananas.

AUNT HATTIE

Bananas are good for you, Casey.

CASEY

Books are good for me, but I don't want to eat them neither.

AUNT HATTIE

Either, and if you're not going to eat breakfast, you can march right back to your room and read a book.

CASEY

I already read those books.

AUNT HATTIE
        (looking skeptical)
Oh, really?
        (She turns to ALEX for
        confirmation.)

ALEX
        (trying with some difficulty
        to swallow a mouthful of
        stale cereal)
It's true, Aunt Hattie. Casey's a really, fast reader. She's avid.
        (She gives AUNT HATTIE a
        self-satisfied look, as if
        ready for her vocabulary to
        be complimented.)

                    AUNT HATTIE
          (humphs)
Well then, you can read the books
in The Boys' Room.

                    CASEY
I've read those too.

                    AUNT HATTIE
          (looks to ALEX again for
          confirmation)
Is this so?

                    ALEX
          (nods)
She finished the last one this
morning.
          (pauses before adding with
          slightly less confidence)
She's avid.

                    AUNT HATTIE
So you said. Well, Casey. What
would you like for breakfast?

                    CASEY
          (without hesitation)
Pie.

                    AUNT HATTIE
          (mutters under her breath)
Oh, for crying out loud.
          (to CASEY)
Pie?

                    CASEY
          (haughtily)
Yes.
          (hesitates just a moment
          before adding)
And ice cream.

                    AUNT HATTIE
Pie and ice cream, is it?

     (CASEY nods.)

                    AUNT HATTIE
          (marveling)
And you really read all those
books?

     (CASEY nods.)

                    AUNT HATTIE
I'll make a deal with you, Casey.
You tell me about the last book
you read and you can have pie—and
a banana—for breakfast.

                    CASEY
          (She considers this for a
          moment, then reaches for a
          banana. In a blasé tone she
          explains.)
So there are these three brothers
and they're all named Karamazov.

          (BLACKOUT)

Dear Jillian,

I see what you mean when you write about things being "lively." They are definitely "lively" here. The first week was a little rough, but we all seem to be settling in. Alex is delighted with her "summer chore." I'll let her tell you about it when she next writes.

Regarding Casey, we've had a change of plans. You never told me what a remarkable reader she is. I was telling my neighbor (you remember Goldie) about it and we think she might just be a child prodigy, which would certainly explain some of her behavioral challenges and other idiosyncrasies.

I've decided to take the girls to Boston tomorrow to have Casey's IQ tested. It'll take a full day, so Goldie will come with us to keep Alex company. I think she plans to take her to visit some of the tourist attractions the young people of today seem to like so much.

Casey doesn't take as keen an interest in chores as her sister, so we've compromised. Instead of helping around the house, she's opted to read. I insisted she also do some writing. Her first assignment is enclosed. It's certainly fervent.

Aunt Hattie

The Lonely Banana
by K.C. Roy

Once upon a time there was a little girl and boy named Jane and Jack. They were twins. Every morning their mother would say (just before school). "Go get a piece of fruit from the fruit basket."

The fruit basket was a nice, beautiful, woven basket always filled with fruit. Jane liked oranges and Jack liked apples. They both hated bananas.

One day, there were: no apples, no oranges, no peaches, no grapes, no cherries, no pineapple and no cantaloupe.

The only thing left was a sad lonely banana. If you know how the kids felt, then you will know the banana felt worse. He was sad because all his friends were gone. Then he heard a voice.

"I brought home some fruit."

All of a sudden, the basket was being filled with all kinds of fruit, so the banana was happy.

As for the children, they still hated bananas.

Dear Aunt Hattie, Alex and Casey *

It is a cloudy Saturday morning and I wanted to take a moment to write you before the various activities of the day distract me. Things have been pretty quiet here. Jillian (Mom) has been taking the dog to obedience training, with minimal results.

Sammy has been writing a great deal. She's very proud and asked me to include her most recent work titled "My Write-about-Things-and-People Book." I hope you all enjoy it. If you do, I imagine you won't have to wait too long for the next installment. She's quite prolific. When she's not playing with the dog, she's

---

* This is Dad's weather report and a confession that he and Mom have completely lost their ability to control Sammy. Apparently she's writing on the side of the house and they don't even care! Things have really gone wild back there. Who would have known that Casey and I have been the ones to keep mayhem at bay? The last bit is about Einstein and counting but I won't even try to figure out what that means.

writing everywhere—even on the side of the house.

Oh well. I try to remind myself of Albert Einstein, who said: "Not everything that can be counted counts and not everything that counts can be counted." There's probably a sermon in there somewhere—maybe even two.

I hope you are treasuring this time together. Remember to treat one another with care.

Much love and God bless,

Walt (Dad)

My write-about-things-and-people book by Sammy Roy!*

i will tell you some things we make for gifts when you won't have to pay! it's okay because even this list is free for you!

1. a box made out of popsicle sticks! you can use the box to put things into!
2. a card made out of paper! you can give the card to someone special! like yourself!
3. a book made out of cardboard and paper! you can draw a picture with crayons and pencils too!
4. a picture of your favorite person! me!

---

* I don't know why Dad got so worked up about this. It certainly doesn't seem all that impressive to me. Perhaps after having Casey, he just had really low expectations. Also, what kind of cockamamie list has only nine things on it?

5. Puppets made out of socks, buttons and yarn and vice versa!*

6. a necklace made out of string or yarn!

7. a paper sailboat made out of paper!

8. a bell made out of a yogurt container and yarn!

9. a coat or scarf or mittens or hat made out of cloth and a needle and thread!

---

* I have no idea how Sammy came upon this expression, but she took to it like a pig to mud, as my mother would say. In case your Latin is a little rusty, *vice versa* means in reverse order. In other words, Sammy is saying that puppets can be made out of socks *and also* socks can be made out of puppets. Now I'm not sure when you last plopped a pair of marionettes on your feet, but for me, this is completely nonsensical. And this is just the beginning.

Dear Mom, Dad, Sammy & Roy's Regret,

Whew! A lot has been happening here in Maine! Guess what my chore is. Cooking! Aunt Hattie said I can do ALL the cooking—breakfast, lunch and dinner—for the ENTIRE summer. It's a good thing too, because otherwise Casey might starve and I mean actually STARVE. Aunt Hattie says in Olden Times, girls my age did all the cooking and she said she thought I was a "smart enough cookie" to figure it out. You get it? COOKie? Ha ha ha. Aunt Hattie gets funnier every day.

Guess what. Yesterday, Aunt Hattie's neighbor (you remember Goldie) took me to Boston. We spent the whole day seeing all there was to see. And I got cotton candy—my favorite! Casey didn't get to go because she read all of Aunt Hattie's books, so Aunt Hattie had to take her to the doctor!

I need to go now. My roast needs basting. Do you know what that means? I do too!

I love you and miss you all sooooo much.

Sincerely,
A. Roy

P.S. I gave Casey The Boys' Room because she was so sad and I felt bad for her. She still feels sad, but I feel better!

P.P.S. X X X O O O O

P.P.P.S. Did you know X and O stand for hugs and kisses? I did too!

P.P.P.P.S. The hugs are for all of you but the kisses are only for the humans. I'm not going to kiss Roy's Regret. Eeew! I'm not going to make that mistake again!

Dear Alex,

I'm glad you are making yourself useful around the house. I've started collecting recipes so you can be just as useful when you come home. Sammy misses you a lot, as do your father and I. I'm not so sure about Roy's Regret. I think he may be a little offended you didn't want to kiss him. I suppose that's the price of having standards.

Love,

JR

Dear Diary,

I've discovered there is something worse than Aunt Hattie not paying attention to me. Guess what that is. It's Aunt Hattie being PREOCCUPIED with me. It's unbearable. My only consolation is that I don't have to do any chores and all I have to do is read and get even smarter. Plus, she's making Alex cook for me.

I told Alex that she was like the servant and I was the highborn aristocrat and Alex said she spit on my food. The joke's on her though, because I swapped my food with Aunt Hattie's!!!

Last week, Aunt Hattie kidnapped me again and took me to see a bunch of scientists. They looked like they were examining a paramecium and I WAS IT!!!

Only 42 days left. I tried carving it in the wall, but it's made of plaster so it just fell apart. Why is this house and everything in it so old??? I would tell you how many minutes I have left but it would just depress me more and I would have to jump out the window.

Finally not starving at least,
K.C. the Highborn Aristocrat

P.S. I actually do have another consolation because the tests came back and it turns out I am the smart one.

P.P.S. An update on the window—it's old so of course it doesn't open. I will need to devise another way to escape this prison.

Dear GREAT Aunt Hattie,

It sounds like this is quickly becoming a summer you will never forget. I'm not surprised Casey is a strong reader. She's had a lot of practice during time-outs. If it turns out she's a genius, we'll be sure to give you credit. Do you want a finder's fee? Will you accept a child instead?

Love,

JR

dear alex and casey,

how are you? how is aunt hattie? i am fine besept✻ i am sooo sad because i miss you sooo much.

yesterday, mom needed to buy me a bucket because i cried so many tears. i think today she'll need to buy me an even bigger bucket.

i miss you so much! when are you coming home?

all the best!

sammy roy!

P.S. alex, i gave roy's regret a kiss for you anyway. you were right! it was disgusting.

✻ She means "except" and before you start thinking about how cute this was, I'm here to tell you it wasn't cute at all. It made her sound like a doofus, which of course I never told her because I'm a considerate person who cares about people's feelings. Plus, I didn't have to because Casey took care of it. She's an entirely *different* class of human being.

Dear Casey,

Stairs are hard for worms. ❖

Love,

JR

❖ I have no idea what this means and I can only assume Mom was being what she called "creative," which is different from the regular word "creative" because she says it while wiggling her fingers and raising her eyebrows. In the interest of full disclosure, you should know the original postcard included a pencil drawing of a worm with a beret and a mustache. I can only presume that meant he was French.

Dear Diary,

Today I was reading one of Aunt Hattie's old diaries and I came upon some disastrous news! She DOES like Alex better and she has all along! I feel sooooo betrayed.

Just when I thought I would finally have someone on my side, this happens! I think I was born under an unlucky star that then crapped all over me.

The worst part is that I can't confront the traitor. I try to hint at it but she's not picking up on what I'm dishing out. I don't know what to do!!!! If I confront her outright, she'll think I'm a snoop, which I'm not! I can't help it if God gave me a curious mind!

Here is my evidence:

8.4.72 (Copenhagen)

Arrived this morning and took a cab to the cheap hostel where Jillian wanted to stay. Fortunately, it was full of tramps and we were able to stay at a nicer place. One would think she'd be more protective of her one-year-old, but far be it from me to criticize.

Little Alex travels exceptionally well. She eats Vienna sausages out of the can, milk when we have it (otherwise apple juice), and bits of whatever we manage to find. She also loves beer. She sleeps in the corner, in a bed, on the floor, on the couch protected by chairs, anywhere. She is a very happy baby.✱

✱ I would have been a happy baby too if I was drunk and sleeping in a corner with a can of processed meat. On OPPOSITE DAY!!! P.S. See—Alex isn't the only one who can write something stupid at the bottom of the page!

The diary is from when she took Alex, Mom and Dad to Europe, which is also totally NOT fair. Most of it is in code about some guy named Chivas Regal. Like this part:

8.12.72 (Bad Kreuznach)
   12:30am: Ran out of ice on Chivas Regal.
   12:45am: In ice! Chivas Regal gone.
   1:00am: Out of ice, Chivas Regal and good cards.
   2:30: To bed.

Who is Chivas Regal?* And for that matter, who was Bad Kreuznach?** And most importantly, who would name their kid "Bad" and not expect them to grow up and BE bad??? It's like he didn't even have a

---

* It's a kind of whisky.

** It's a town in Germany.

fighting chance. Then he falls in love with Aunt Hattie (who was probably beautiful and nice in Olden Times), who then ditches him for this other clown. How can I find out these answers? Aha! I have an idea. I am so lucky to be smart AND pretty!

Plan A: Trick Alex into asking

Plan B: Ask Goldie

Plan C: Hypnotize Aunt Hattie to find out information and brainwash her into liking me more than she likes Alex!!! Ha! Ha! Ha!

Wish me luck!

K.C. the Wily

Dear Casey,

Would you like to study Animal Husbandry? ⁜

Love,

JR

⁜If you don't know what "Animal Husbandry" is, then you need to look it up on your own because it's disgusting and there's no way I'm going to tell you.

P.S. I'll give you a hint. Mom says it involves "candlelight and mooooood music."

P.P.S. You get it? "Mooooood music"?

Dear Mom, Dad, Sammy & Roy's Regret,

How are you? I am fine. I can't believe the summer is almost over. It is soooooo much fun at Aunt Hattie's, even if you're not here and Casey is. Ha ha ha. Aunt Hattie lets me do so many things. Do you know what a stock portfolio is? Neither do I, but she sure spends a lot of time talking to me about it.

I've got to go! It's 4:57 and that means I only have three minutes to make Aunt Hattie's Stinger. She's like clockwork! Ha ha ha!

I love you and miss you all soooo much! See you soon!

Sincerely,

A. Roy

Dear Casey,

   Gobblety schmoblety boo. [*]

Love,

JR

---

[*] Believe me, I'd help you out if I could, but the woman is a mystery to me and I have no clue what this is supposed to mean.

Dear Diary,

The woman who claims she's my "mother" keeps writing me these stupid postcards, trying to trick me into writing her back, but I'm too smart for that crap. Not like Alex, who is forever writing blah blah blah home to Sammy, Princess and my "parents." Not me! My thoughts are precious and meant ONLY for me!!!

K.C. the Great

P.S. There is a bird stalking me outside my window. All day long it tweets and tweets. I smack the window to scare it away but it just looks at me with its beady little eyes. I bet he's the one responsible for my window not opening in the first place. I bet he glued it shut with his stinky guamo.✢

✢ She means "guano" as in bird poop. "Guamo" is a city in Tuscany.

dear alex & casey,

how are you? i am fine. i miss you. we are so lonely here without you. where is casey? is she okay? dad and i are worried because she doesn't write.

mom's not worried because she says it's a stage. what's a stage? roy's regret isn't worried either but i think that's probably because he's a dog. if you do see casey, will you tell her i love her and miss her soooo much?

all the best!
sammy roy!

p.s. i drew this bunny for casey because i love her sooo much!

Dear Sammy,

How are you? I am fine. I have matured so much this summer. I think it will be difficult when I go back to school if the adults try to treat me like a kid. Maybe when you are 11, then you can come and stay for the summer with Aunt Hattie. It's definitely a unique experience. Ha ha ha! Just so you know, she could be dead by then and so you probably wouldn't be able to come. I don't say this to scare you because it's just a fact of life.

We are coming home very soon so don't be too sad. Do you want me to bring you a present?

Sincerely,
A. Roy

P.S. Casey says "hi" and she loves you and misses you too!

No I didn't!!! Alex is a big fat liar!!!

Dear Diary,

I'm so sick of these stupid birds! Can't a person get any peace and quiet in this stupid town? I want to buy a gun and shoot all of them in the beak!

K.C. the Furious

P.S. Only four more days until my sentence is up and I'm freeeeee!!!

dear alex & casey,
    we are going to the airport now to
pick you up! i'm sooooooooo excited!
    all the best!
    sammy roy! 🐰

P.S. yes, i do want a present. will you
bring me a maple tree?

P.P.S. just tricking!

Dear Diary,

Gone are those sweet Maine days when I was free to read books, breathe clean air, think deep thoughts and hear the peaceful sounds of birds chirping. It was the only time I've ever been truly happy.* Now, all I hear is Mom nagging, Sammy whining and Dad telling me to try harder to find my better self—whatever the crap that means. To make matters worse, Alex had to come back with me! Will I never be free of her???

Bitterly,

K.C. the Nostalgic

P.S. Mom asked me about getting her postcards and I told her I didn't get anything addressed to "K.C." so I couldn't help her with that one.

---

* I know, I know.

Dear Walter and Jillian,

I imagine things are "lively" at home once again. Is it true that absence makes the heart grow fonder?

Speaking of which, if I ever ask to have the girls for the summer again, please don't let me. Of course, with how exhausted I am, I probably won't be around for another one anyway.

At least I won't die of hunger. Alex made enough food to last me through winter. It's in the freezer — all neatly labeled and packaged. I'm not sure, but it may also be alphabetized. You might want to take her to see someone about that.

Aunt Hattie

Christmastime Is Fruit & Wine

Alex: still 11

Casey: still 9

Sammy: still 5

Roy's Regret: a year and a season older than "no clue"

Mom & Dad: 99% old and 1% young

Aunt Hattie: She witnessed The Big Bang while drinking a Stinger and smoking a Pall Mall so that's how old she is!

Dear Diary,

Today one good thing happened. I told Sammy that Santa probably wouldn't be coming because the reindeer were sick! She is so dumb! Not as dumb as Alex. I think Alex is ignominious.*

Rebelliously and brilliantly,

K.C. the Original

---

* I think she must mean "ignorant" since "ignominious" means "shameful" as in the ignominious behavior of talking behind your sister's back! And don't say that's exactly what I'm doing, because what I'm doing is an exposé, which is an entirely different matter altogether thank you very much!

Underroos

That Christmas brought the Underoos craze.❖ We each received a set from Grandma Esther. Casey and I were Supergirl with bikini tops and bottoms. Sammy was Wonder Woman, with a tank top instead. The goal of the game was to keep two oranges under your top, rearrange the living room furniture and chase one another without touching the floor or losing your boobs.

❖ Underoos were cheap, polyester underwear designed to make us look like knock-off superheroes. Their slogan was: Underoos! Underwear that's fun to wear! Turns out, they were right.

The Oldest Profession

Not long after Casey and I returned from our time at Aunt Hattie's, we (as part of the negotiation for a temporary ceasefire) decided to put on a talent show for our parents. Our grand finale was a song Aunt Hattie taught us from Olden Times. We taught it to Sammy and designed our costumes, which basically involved putting stuffed animals in our underwear so our skirts would pop out in back.[❖] And for the icing on the cake, we added choreography.[❖❖] This was the song:

Put on your old gray bustle,[❖❖❖]
Stick your fanny out and hustle,
For tomorrow, the rent is coming due.
While the bees are making honey,
Let your fanny make some money.
If you can't make five, take two!

❖ I'll admit, it wasn't too fancy, but this also wasn't Broadway, for crying out loud.

❖❖ Before you get too impressed, the "choreography" was basically a combination of synchronized line-kicking and shaking our butts with wild abandon.

❖❖❖ A "bustle" is some kind of mechanical contraption women in Olden Times would wear under their skirts to make their butts look big. Why? Your guess is as good as mine.

We finished our performance with a gigantic flourish and jazz-hands. As my father's jaw dropped, my mother gave us an enthusiastic standing ovation.

"And here you were worried about Aunt Hattie's influence," she chided my father.

He stood reluctantly and clapped half-heartedly. "Yes, and now my girls know about The Oldest Profession."✢

My mother shrugged and said, "Well, they should at least have options."✢✢

✢ If you don't know what that means, it's a euphemism for being a carpenter. Casey says, "If you don't know what a euphemism is, you're dumber than you look." Also, if you don't believe me, you could ask an adult. But if you do, be sure not to tell them you heard it from me because I will SO get sent to my room for that. By the way, if you don't know what a "fanny" is, you should probably get off it and go buy a dictionary.

✢✢ I have to give my mom credit on this one. No matter our aspirations, she wanted to make sure we weren't hampering our own imagination. In my case, she certainly accomplished this. For much of my childhood, when adults would ask me what I wanted to be when I grew up, I would answer confidently, "I either want to be President of the United States or a cocktail waitress."

Dear Aunt Hattie,

How are you? We are all fine here. Is it true you are getting a cat? That's sure exciting. Everyone loves cats, unless of course you're a dog but you're not a dog so probably you are fine!

Yesterday, we performed the song you taught us and we were a huge hit. Mom loved it so much she was almost crying. Dad loved it so much he is going to have some words with you!

Guess what! Today Sammy and Mom ate a whole stick of butter! I know! I couldn't believe it either but it sure was true.

Dad said, "Where's the butter?"

And Sammy said, "We ate it!"

Then Dad said, "With what?"

And Sammy said, "With each other!"

It was so funny I laughed and laughed.

Sincerely,

Alex

Another One-Sided Conversation

Walt (*answering telephone*): Good afternoon, Roy Residence—Aunt Hattie! It's so nice to hear your—

Pause.

Walt: Butter? You don't say.

Long pause.

Walt: Yes, I suppose that's—

Very long pause.

Walt: Well, I sure appreciate you letting me—

Short pause.

Walt: Okay then. Take care, Aunt Hattie. Thanks for calling. We love you.

Mr. Chivas Regal

That winter, for some reason, Casey became obsessed with Chivas Regal, which is apparently some kind of hard liquor. But there was absolutely no way to convince her of this.

"Casey," I tried to explain, in my most patient and authoritative tone. "I've told you."

"Don't patronize me, Alex."

"I'm not patronizing you. I'm trying to benefit you with my wisdom."

"You're a known liar."

"Shut up!"

"You shut up! Don't try to trick me. I'm too smart for you, dumbo."

"No," I said. "You just *think* you're too smart for me. That's not the same thing at all. If you were smarter than I, then you would know Chivas Regal is not a person. He is alcohol."

"No he isn't."

"Even Mom told you."

Casey just looked at me with a dubious expression.

"Fine," I conceded. "I'll admit she's not the most reliable source of information, but Dad said it too, remember? That time you wanted to 'invite' Mr. Chivas Regal to dinner and Dad sent you to your room?"

"It wasn't for that!" Casey snapped. "It was because I insulted Mom's food."*

"It was for both."

"It still doesn't matter what you say. I can recognize a conspiracy when I smell one and you all stink of it!"

"Who's 'you all'?" I demanded exasperatedly.

Casey huffed, threw her hands on her hips and rolled her eyes.** "You know perfectly well who I'm talking about."

"About whom I'm talking," I corrected automatically, earning a pinch.

"MOM!" I yelled, earning a harder pinch.

Casey lowered her voice and I felt like I was talking to the mafia's most ruthless hit man. "Now, you listen to me, you little brat, and you listen good. I don't know what kind of scheme you and Aunt Hattie and Chivas Regal have cooked up, but I'm not fooled for a minute."

"But Case—ouch!"

---

* When Casey had suggested we invite Mr. Chivas Regal to dinner, she didn't express it in the most appropriate way. I'm not sure what her exact words were, but it was something to the effect of, "We should get that Mr. Chivas Regal down here so Aunt Hattie can get her squeaky wheel oiled—if you know what I'm talking about—and then she won't be so mean. But when he does come, we can't serve him this Arvon crap."

** Just so you know, this is pretty much her primary stance throughout the entire book. A distant second is stomping into her room and slamming the door. There is no third.

She glared and whispered, "I'm onto you clowns," before grabbing the dog, stomping off to her room and slamming the door.

dear diary,

casey roy is driving me bonkers! yesterday, she told me she could digest metal. i told her that wasn't true and she said it was and i said it wasn't and she said it was <u>so</u> and i said it was <u>not</u> and you probably know how that went for a while.

but then, i told her, "oh yeah! well i can digest ice! it just melts in my stomach!"

she sure didn't see that one coming!

all the best!

sammy roy!

P.S. guess what! we got a cat!

Dear Aunt Hattie,

How are you? I am fine. Dad just told me you arrived in Florida safely! Yay! I must say, I was a little worried. Partly because of your driving—no offense, but I think we both know that's true. Ha ha ha. But mostly because you took the cat with you in the car. Dad said you named him Kitty Kit. Sammy wants to know what his other names are. I tried to explain it to her, but you know how that goes.

Speaking of which, we got a cat too! His name is Fatty Catty except that Dad just calls him The Cat. Maybe he and Kitty Kit can have a get-together sometime. Does Kitty Kit have many friends? Fatty Catty doesn't. Mom says he's still working on his social skills. I can tell you one thing. His eating skills are excellent. That's why he got his name!

Have fun training Kitty Kit to "freshen your drink." Ha ha ha.

Sincerely,

Alex

P.S. I forgot to tell you I miss you!

P.P.S. I miss you!

To Santa claus,

   how are you? i think i'm very well. i hope the reindeer are not sick. merry christmas and happy new year. good bye. i love you!

   all the best!
   sammy roy!

P.S. don't Forget to write me, or vice versa!

Dear Diary,

Finally! I have a friend to call my own. For Christmas, the people who pay for things bought me my very own cat. I've named her Snowball, which Alex says is a stupid name because he's yellow and a boy. I told her SHE was yellow and a boy and then Dad spent FOREVER explaining why calling someone yellow was offensive. I told him about this little thing I liked to call The First Amendment and that's why I'm in my room right now. I can't believe I'm only nine and already a political prisoner. The good news is I already had Snowball in my dresser drawer so now I have company even though they think they put me in Solitary Confinement. Looks like the joke is on them. Ha!

Befriended at last,

K.C. the Persecuted

Opening Presents

The deal with Christmas presents was that we could each open one gift the night before. After church, we'd rush home to make our selection.*

Casey, despite her promise from the previous year, would always ruin it, because the fun part was the element of surprise. However, since Grandma Esther always gave each of us the same thing, if Casey chose first, which she always did since she complained incessantly, she would make a big production out of trying to decide and then go ahead and pick a Grandma Esther present after all.

We should have known better than to get our hopes up, and Christmas Eve just became an annual reminder of what suckers we were. As if we needed an annual reminder. Casey pretty much told us that every day anyway.

---

* We would spend the week before Christmas "inspecting" the presents. Removing tape took forever so it was much easier once we got Fatty Catty. At first, we'd just tease him with the present until he swiped at it enough for us to get a good peek. Then Casey discovered a better way. Instead we'd hold him so we could rake his claws over the gift. It was much more efficient and probably Fatty Catty didn't mind since, if we weren't using him that way, we'd be playing *Operation*, which consisted of tying him to the coffee table and using kitchen utensils as implements for our varied medical procedures. Of course, this resulted in cat hair in the food because we only wanted to be doctors and everyone knows it's the nurse's job to wash the tools and put them back in the drawer.

COVETING

───────────────────

A Play in One Act

by

Alex Roy

TIME: Christmas, 1982

SETTING: We are in the brightly
            lit dining room of the
            ROY home. There is a
            large window in the
            center with bookshelves
            on either side. A dog's
            tail peeks out from
            beneath the tablecloth.

AT RISE: The ROY family is having
            an animated Sunday
            Dinner. The parents,
            WALT and JILLIAN, sit at
            either end of the table.
            ALEX, the oldest
            daughter, sits centered
            and across from her
            sisters, SAMMY, who is
            feeding the dog, and
            CASEY, who is wearing a
            tiara.

JILLIAN
Well, goils. What did you learn in
choych today?

ALEX	CASEY
(proudly)	(drolly)
The ten	God. Pass the
commandments.	potatoes.

SAMMY
(contributes excitedly)
I learned they put Jesus in
waddling clothes and played him
out of danger.

(JILLIAN and WALT exchange a
smile.)

(WALT passes potatoes to
CASEY.)

SAMMY
(looking concerned)
What's "waddling"?

WALT
I believe it's "swaddling," Sammy.
They put Jesus in swaddling
clothes and laid him in a manger.

(SAMMY looks confused and
starts to repeat her
question.)

                    JILLIAN
It means to wrap something tightly
in cloth, Sammy.

          (Sammy looks a little less
          confused.)

                    ALEX
Like when we play The Sushi Game
and I make Sammy Maki.

          (Sammy nods in satisfaction,
          then grins.)

          (CASEY takes a heaping
          spoonful and reaches for
          another.)

                    WALT
Casey, there's plenty. Why don't
you finish that first before you
take more.

                    ALEX
Yeah, Casey. Waste not, want not.

                    WALT
          (automatically, as if he's
          said it a million times)
Alex, don't aggravate your sister.

                    ALEX
          (looking contrite)
Yes, Pa.

    (CASEY puts the spoon back
    and glares at WALT, who has
    turned away and so misses the
    look.)

              ALEX
    (reaching for potatoes)
What's "coveting"?

             JILLIAN
    (She half laughs/half chokes
    and reaches for water.)
What's that, Alex?

              ALEX
    (not noticing her mother's
    response)
Coveting. Reverend Floyd mentioned
it this morning in the sermon. He
was talking about the Ten
Commandments. You know, "You shall
not make false idols. You shall
not have any other gods above Me."

             CASEY
    (mutters)
How about, "You shall shut up."
    (she takes a huge bite of
    potatoes)

             JILLIAN
Let's keep things civil, toots.

ALEX
(admonishes)
Yeah, Casey.

CASEY
(mimics)
Yeah, Casey.

WALT
Casey, your spoon is not a shovel.

(CASEY glares at ALEX, who
promptly takes an
exceptionally small and
dainty bite of her food. In
response, CASEY takes another
exceptionally large bite of
her food.)

(ALEX begins inching over so
as to be directly across from
CASEY. Everyone but CASEY
appears oblivious.)

CASEY
(mouths silently)
Bring it on, sister.

WALT
(professorially)
You know, a little known fact
about Mount Sinai, where Moses
received the commandments—

CASEY
(wincing)
Ouch! Alex kicked me!

WALT
Alex?

ALEX
It was an accident. I think I have a nervous tick.
(She nods toward CASEY.)
From all the stress.

CASEY
(mutters angrily)
I'll give you a nervous tick.

WALT
(sighs)
Casey.

CASEY
(indignantly)
What? It's the season of giving.

SAMMY
(in a dead-on impersonation of a southern Baptist preacher)
Je-sus-ah…is the ah-rea-son-ah…for the ah-sea-son-ah.

(WALT and JILLIAN laugh.)

(CASEY glares.)

(ALEX laughs and sprays the milk she's been drinking.)

(CASEY laughs uproariously at ALEX.)

(ALEX glares.)

                    WALT
          (He composes himself and
          clears his throat.)
As to your question, Alex…I
believe it derives its meaning
from French, meaning "to lust
after."

          (JILLIAN looks at WALT with
          a raised eyebrow.)

                    WALT
          (looking a little affronted)
What? I thought we agreed if they
can handle the question, they can
handle the answer.

                    JILLIAN
They can. Can you?

          (It just now seems to occur
          to WALT that he may have
          gotten himself into some
          uncomfortable territory.)

                    ALEX
          (unconcerned and undeterred)
I get the other commandments.
          (She puts her fork down to
          count on her fingers.)
You shall not kill.

                    CASEY
          (under her breath)
Unless necessary.

                    JILLIAN
          (with a sideways glance and a
          warning tone)
Casey.

                    CASEY
          (with the same tone)
Mo-om.

                    ALEX
And you shall not steal.

                    CASEY
          (under her breath)
Unless necessary.

                    JILLIAN
          (with a warning tone)
Casey.

                    CASEY
          (with the same tone)
Mo-om.

                    ALEX
And you shall not commit adultery.

                    CASEY
          (under her breath)
Unless—
          (grimaces in disgust)
—ew!

                    JILLIAN
          (under her breath)
Didn't see that coming, did you?

          (CASEY glares at JILLIAN)

                    JILLIAN
          (smiling, handing her the
          dish)
More potatoes, Casey?

                    SAMMY
What's adultery?

          (JILLIAN raises another
          amused eyebrow at WALT.)

                    ALEX
And, of course, honor thy mother
and father.

          (CASEY wants desperately to
          make a sarcastic rejoinder
          but she has just taken a huge
          bite of potatoes.)

                    173

                    WALT
          (grateful for a new topic)
Now, that one's my favorite!
          (SAMMY takes some food from
          her plate and gives it to
          ROY'S REGRET)

                    JILLIAN
          (in a warning tone)
Sammy.

                    SAMMY
          (in the same tone and looking
          at the dog)
Roy's Regret.
          (She grins at JILLIAN who
          can't help but smile back.)

                    ALEX
But there was a bunch of stuff
about coveting. You shall not
covet your neighbor's—

                    JILLIAN
It means wanting something you
shouldn't.

                    SAMMY
So Roy's Regret is coveting our
dinner?

                    JILLIAN
Precisely.

                    WALT
         (absentmindedly, to himself)
Or perhaps from Latin? From
cupiditat? I think that's right.
         (He stands up, takes the
         napkin from his lap and sets
         it next to his plate. He
         moves to the bookcase
         and begins looking while
         mumbling incoherently.)

                    CASEY
         (wincing dramatically)
Ouch!

         WALT   JILLIAN
(reading book)   (sighs)
Alex.   Alex.

                    ALEX
         (screeching)
I didn't do anything this time!

         (CASEY smirks at ALEX.)

         (ALEX glares at CASEY.)

                    WALT
         (nodding with satisfaction)
Yes. Latin. Cupiditat, which
relates to Cupid, the god of
desire. It means to—
         (quickly closes book and
         returns it to the shelf)

                    WALT (cont.)
Well, never mind. It's what your
mother said.

          (There's a thump and ROY'S
          REGRET whines in pain.)

          (ALEX is horrorstricken.)

                    CASEY
          (whispers accusingly)
Dog-kicker.

                    SAMMY
          (lifting her head in
          interest)
Dog-licker? Alex, you told me you
gave that up years ago.

          (ALEX gets ready to bolt.)

                    JILLIAN
          (dispassionately)
Sit down, Alex.

                    ALEX
          (imploringly)
But I—

                    WALT
          (motions to her full plate)
Yes, Alex. You haven't even
finished your food.

                    CASEY
          (shows off her clean plate
          and stands up to leave)
Well, I'm done.
          (to WALT, sweetly)
May I be excused?

     (WALT nods his permission.)

                    CASEY
          (whispers to ALEX)
Bet you're wishin' you took some
of those big bites now, aren't
you?

     (ALEX starts to rise again.)

     WALT   JILLIAN
Sit down, Alex.   Sit down, Alex.

                    ALEX
But she—

                    JILLIAN
What was that bit about honoring
your mother and father?

                    ALEX
          (sits, disconsolate)
Yes, Ma.

               (BLACKOUT)

Dear Jesus,

I want to set your mind at ease about all this coveting business. According to Dad, it's really important. Now, if I were you, I'd be more worried about all the war and suffering, but Mom keeps telling me I shouldn't tell you how to do your job, so I guess I'll just keep my opinion to myself on that subject.

Anyway, in case you were worried about me coveting my neighbor's wife, I wanted to let you know that my neighbor, Dr. Michael, has a wife, but Mom says she's too old for me so I think it's probably not going to be much of a problem.

Our other neighbor is Mr. Fitzsimmons. His wife is mean and always yells at us to get out of her damn garden so I think we can both agree coveting her isn't too likely either.

And since we are already on the subject of coveting, I know there wasn't anything in your commandments about coveting your neighbor's dog, but you might want to revise that. It's just a suggestion. I'm not trying to tell you how to do your job, but Mom talks to Rufus a lot! I mean A LOT! We have Roy's Regret, but sometimes I think that isn't enough for her, because the kinds of conversations Mom has with Roy's Regret are usually related to poop.

Well, Jesus, I know you like confessions so I do have one for you. I am definitely coveting Casey's music box she got from Grandma Esther for Christmas, mostly because I can't find mine. I wanted to ask you, if I took it and put it in my room, does it count as stealing since it is still in the same house? I'm not sure if you can see through walls, but my room and Casey's room are right across the hall from each other. If I take it I will no longer be coveting it because I will have it and then Casey would be the one coveting it, but I would forgive her because, as you know, I'm just that kind of person. I'm pretty sure that's how it works but please let me know if that's not the case.

Sincerely,
A. Roy

P.S. I also don't understand why you are worried about me coveting my neighbor's ass, but Mom says I'll have plenty of time to learn about that when I'm older.

The Alex Shrine

For a long time, Casey kept all her dresses in a pile on the floor, because she had a different use for her closet. Along with a bunch of pillows (many of which came from my room), there was a cardboard box covered by the polyester (and therefore highly flammable) scarf Aunt Hattie had given my mom one year. On the box were candles, incense, flowers and two Barbie dolls. One was dressed in a piece of fabric cut from Casey's Easter dress. The other had so much duct tape wrapped around it that Barbie looked pregnant on both sides.

Behind the box was a large picture she had painted. In it, two girls—one skinny with blonde curly hair and one plump with straight brown hair—held hands and smiled. In front of the box were a bunch of random objects, including the jewelry box Grandma Esther had given *me* for Christmas. It was positioned alongside Casey's. On the other side were the broken remains of a sculpture I had made in art class and which I had thrown at Casey a few weeks earlier.

Taped to the walls were a bunch of pictures of the two of us when we spent a day at Volunteer Park with our parents. We certainly appeared happy, wearing our OshKosh B'gosh overalls and putting marigolds in each other's hair. Above the pictures was a sign that read, "Happier Times."

Dear Diary,

I was worried about coveting but now I know all about pilfering! I went into Casey's room to take her jewelry box and I found a whole bunch of my stuff piled in her closet! There were also some candles and some stupid picture Casey had drawn of her and her fat imaginary friend.

I told Mom it was a fire hazard and that Casey was a thief. So she and Casey had a talk. I listened outside the door but I could only hear Casey sniffling and Mom telling her a story about The God of How Things Ought to Be.

Other than telling her the story, Mom didn't punish Casey at all! She just talked to her about "feelings" and taught her how to use the fire extinguisher.

What is this world coming to?
Sincerely,
A. Roy

Dear Diary,

Just like Bad Kreuznach, I've been pigeon-holed. I was reading Alex's diary and she thinks I'm just a pilferer. My feelings weren't hurt at first, but then I looked it up. It means a stealer! How can she understand me so little? Why can't things be the way they used to be, when we were best friends and kindred spirits?

When I talked with Mom, I explained what kind of sister Alex was in my Happiness Closet. She said she understood and things just worked like that sometimes. Then, we talked about how things ought to be.

She was a small comfort and I made a special point of telling her so.

Bereft and blamed,

K.C. the Pilferer

The Voice

Alex: age 12

Casey: age 10

Sammy: age 6

Roy's Regret: classic

Mom & Dad: old but no one has the heart to tell them

Aunt Hattie: Let me put it to you this way. She was God's secretary.

A Close Shave

Dad had a beard and Mom didn't shave, so heaven only knows where Casey got the razor. Regardless, my parents came home one day and she had shaved off one of her eyebrows, which gave her a look of perpetual skepticism.

My father was pretty mad. He told her she could shave one more thing and it gosh darn better be the other eyebrow.

She shaved the cat.

Mom and Dad,

Guess what! This is your daughter Sammy Roy! While you were away, I taught myself to use the typewriter!

Wake me up when you get home so I can say "hello" and vice versa! Okay?

All the best!

Sammy Roy!

P.S. I'm in the living room.

P.P.S. On the couch.

Gigantic Footprints
by Sammy Roy!

One day, I was in the woods. I put my foot down to take another step and…I stepped right into a gigantic footprint! It was shaped like a tulip lying down on the ground. It was as long as me! I followed the footprint into a cave but when I got in the cave, I saw that it was just my sister, Casey Roy, playing a trick on me!

She had used my dad's false bear foot. As soon as I got into the cave, she was laughing like crazy. And then she stopped as soon as I saw her. That was how I found out it was her. Because I've heard that crazy laugh a hundred times before!

The End

Zanzibar

Casey and I loved camping. While Mom and Dad were setting up the tent, we'd get our story straight, argue a little over the names we'd use and head out.

"We're going to the playground!" we'd call in unison.

"Take your sister!" my parents would call back in unison.

At the playground, we'd take an initial survey to assess the scene and the kids, then make some final adjustments to our strategy. After telling Sammy to keep her mouth shut this time, the show would begin.

"Febelian swu tey mo frilapantaora?" I'd ask Casey in my best Arabic-French-Hebrew accent.

"Doishty fan bu camorides," she'd reply in her German-Dutch preference.

We'd laugh at the "joke" she just made and continue our conversation until a kid approached us.

"Where are you from?" would always be the first question.

Usually, I'd answer while Casey cast them a look of utter disdain and superiority. She was very good at that.

"We are from Zanzibar!" I'd say, rolling my "r"s.

"Far out," the kid would say, or something equally as pedestrian. "I'm from Rhode Island. What's your name?"

"I am Arianna," Casey would interrupt—whether or not she had fairly won the name.

I'd then choose the second best. "I am Barbie," I'd say, again with a rolling "r."

Casey would point to a silent and smiling Sammy and (in her thickest Eastern-European accent) announce, "This here is Jane."

Sammy would start to say something and Casey would pinch-hug her.*

"She is deaf," I'd explain.

Casey would smile and add, "And also dumb."

---

* For those of you who don't have siblings, this is a strategy whereby one sibling feigns a loving or protective hug, while at the same time pinching the underside of the other sibling's arm. And if you don't know how much it hurts to be pinched there, you are surely an only child.

Budda Budda

Once, Sammy wasn't so silent. She must have watched us play enough times to pick up the rules, which may have seemed simple in design but which required great finesse in execution:

1. Say whatever nonsense you can concoct in whatever accent you can muster.
2. Throw in some tone variations and flailing hand motions so your gibberish resembles an exciting and robust conversation.
3. Be sure to stop once in a while to insert an English word.

"Fushtalana pifticoruna lulatula," I said—this time in something akin to Italian.

"Calabrini, rigatoni, sarsaparilla, hobby-knobby," Casey replied in a derisive and snobby tone before inserting, "United States," and finishing with "grunievity schmopelyt topya!"

We collapsed into gales of laughter. It's true. Casey and I never got along so well as when we didn't know what the other person was saying.

"Budda, budda, budda."

Casey and I whipped our heads around to see the worst-case scenario. Sammy, in spite of explicit orders and threats, was trying to play.

"Budda, budda!" she insisted.

This was abysmal! Surely, we'd be exposed for the charlatans we were with this goofball botching things up!

We quickly grabbed her, before she could ruin everything, and hauled her back to the campsite.

She waved her arms like an angry cook from an old Italian movie. "BUDDA, BUDDA, BUDDA!"

It was after this so-called "Budda Budda situation," that we discovered Sammy's innate talent for voices. Because, while the words were not at all up to par, the accent was spot on. In fact, after we had a chance to regain our composure (and move campsites), Casey and I recognized the value in what had happened. What was so funny was not this six-year-old trying to imitate her sisters and failing miserably—although that was pretty funny. It was that, if you closed your eyes, she sounded exactly like some 300-pound, spaghetti-wielding, *paisan* direct from Sicily with no layover.

Dear Diary,

I've been practicing my DEEP VOICE that Alex Roy and Casey Roy taught me. Today I used it on Casey Roy! If you'd been there, you would have laughed and laughed. She screamed. Now I keep catching her looking at me with a strange expression on her face. I think I finally impressed my sister Casey Roy and that's for sure!

All the best!

Sammy Roy!

The Voice of Satan

We taught our sweet, cherubic, little sister the gravelly-bass growl of Lucifer himself.

Unfortunately, we must have practiced too openly because when we finally sprang our masterpiece at the dinner table, we didn't exactly get the horrified reaction we were anticipating.

My mother sighed. "Alex, please pass the *pfeffer*. Casey, don't slouch and Sammy, no Satan at the dinner table.

"Yes, ma'am," bellowed our baby sister from the bowels of hell.

Dear Diary,

Today, Alex and I told Sammy we would give her a dollar if she said, "Happy Thanksgiving, Aunt Hattie" in her Satan Voice. Probably, she won't because she's such a wimp, but we have a month until Aunt Hattie visits so we have some time to do some "convincing."

Craftily,

K.C. the Genius

Beer and Vienna Sausages out of the Can

You really have to give credit where credit is due. Casey could tease with merciless precision. Pushing buttons was her forte, no question. One of her all-time favorite pastimes was going to the hallway outside my parents' study (when she knew my mom was trying to work) and slamming her fist into a pillow to simulate sounds of a physical struggle.

"Ow!" she'd screech. "Alex, stop punching me!"

"Alex!" Mom would yell, without even deigning to confirm an assault had been committed. "Don't punch your sister!"

Another strategy would be to harp on something asinine* so incessantly that you'd end up going crazy in frustration. And what made it even more frustrating was how nonsensical it was! For example, one time, she became obsessed with me drinking beer and eating Vienna sausages out of the can.

"Girls," my father would ask. "What do you want for dinner?"

"Alex wants beer and Vienna sausages out of the can," Casey would say sweetly.

---

* I know this sounds like a swear word but it actually isn't. And if you don't believe me, it's not my fault that I have an advanced vocabulary and you don't have a dictionary.

Or when we were playing with the neighborhood kids and one would say, "Do you guys want to play hide and seek?" Casey would reply, "Well, that sure sounds fun to me but I think Alex only wants to drink beer and eat Vienna sausages out of the can."

Or in church, when some old lady would ask what we were learning in school.

"Sammy's learning the alphabet and I'm learning trigonometry and Alex is learning how to drink beer and eat Vienna sausages out of the can."

The evil brilliance imbedded in this plan is that eventually the victim (me) gets so accustomed to it that you start trying to undermine the perpetrator (Casey) by depriving her of your reaction—taking the wind out of her sails, so to speak.

For instance, we were at a restaurant and the waiter asked me what I wanted and Casey looked like she was about to jump in, so I cut her off at the pass by saying in a sarcastic tone, "Gosh, I suppose I *do* want to drink some beer and eat Vienna sausages out of the can. Ha ha ha."

There's a down side. The waiter (or the neighbor or the stewardess or the teacher or the minister or the bus driver or Dad) doesn't know the back story. In the end, I'm the one who sounds stupid (at the very least) and (at worst) like I'm an 12-year-old with a severe alcohol problem and very poor taste in food.

Either way, I'm getting sent to my room and that's for darn sure.

Dear Diary,

Today Jillian Roy took me and Casey Roy to buy new shoes. On the way home Casey got mad. She said to Mom, "I hate you."

Then she threw her new shoes out the window. The car was still moving!

All the best!

Sammy Roy!

P.S. I love my new shoes!

Dear Aunt Hattie,

How are you? I am fine. I have already started working on the beautiful pillow you gave me. I thank you for all your gifts. I have corrected my English teacher's grammar two times but I am not doing as well as I could with your corrections. Please come visit us again soon. I miss you and I thank you again!

Sincerely,

Alex

P.S. These were my grades first quarter:

History = A+

Math = A+

Reading = A+

Science = A+

English = B-

Dear Aunt Hattie,

Guess what. This is your GREAT grand niece Sammy Roy! I disguised my handwriting by learning how to use the typewriting machine! Pretty tricky huh? Jillian Roy, my mom, says that's the advantage of being a "casual parent." Next it's the sewing machine for me! Ouch in advance! Ha ha ha!

Is your cat doing well? If it is, write a letter back to me.

We were outside in the snow and all the lights went out. We couldn't see the house and vice versa! Don't worry. I can see the page because I lit a candle. Walt Roy, my dad, says it makes him nervous to see me play with fire, so I'm staying in my room.

All the best!

Sammy Roy!

P.S. Did you notice I don't have many errors in my letter? This is because Alex Roy, my sister, checked it over for me. She says you are getting too old and tired to correct it yourself.

That's okay. That's what sisters are for!

P.P.S. I thought it might be mean to call you "old and tired" but I asked my sister Casey Roy and she explained it's not considered mean if it's true!

Advice

One day after school, Sammy rushed off the bus and barreled into the house.

Breathless, she told Mom, "I got it! I got it!"

"Good for you, Sammy," my mother said. "Remember, as a member of the fourth estate, you must only use this power for good."

A little while later, Casey stumbled in, having dragged her belongings all the way from school.* "What are you so happy about?" she accused.

My mother pointed to the porch and Casey sighed audibly before stepping back outside to shake all the dirt off. As she came back in, my mother pointed to the pile of dirt Casey had deposited onto the kitchen floor.

"Do I have to?" Casey whined.

"Unfortunately, the maid called in sick today, so yes, Casey, I expect you to clean up your mess."

"But I'm so tired," Casey groaned, collapsing on the floor in a pile of drama (and dirt). "I think I have polo.** I may need an iron lung."

---

* After an "incident" with the bus driver, Casey had to walk to and from school, which my mom said benefited everyone, just in different ways.

** She means polio, which is a disease. Polo, on the other hand, is a game played by rich people who are riding even richer horses. Once again, reading medical journals and not paying attention to details had not served my sister well.

"I'm fresh out of iron lungs, I'm afraid," my mother said drolly. "What I do have for you today is a broom."

Casey grumbled, grabbed the broom and proceeded to "sweep" up the dirt. And by sweep, I mean spread it around the floor so somehow it appeared (in her eyes) as less, even though it had only been dispersed.

"So tell me the whole story, Sammy," my mother said.

Sammy, who was about to bounce out of her shoes with excitement, told Mom about the class newspaper. "So, first I thought I wanted to draw the cartoons and then I changed my mind and I wanted to be the reporter and then I thought of the best job!" She paused to beam with pride. "I'm doing the advice column!"

"That's wonderful, Sammy."

"It's stupid, that's what it is," muttered Casey.

"Mom!" Sammy shouted.

"I'm right here, Sammy." My mother sighed. "I heard her." She gave Casey The Look but Casey just gave her own The Look right back.

"I'm so excited, Mom. Just think—I'll get to advise the entire class!"

Casey stopped sweeping. "I've got some advice for you," she offered.

Sammy, who was always too quick to forgive and forget, cheerfully asked, "What?"

"Why don't you do everyone a favor and put a bag over your head?"

Dear Diary,

Do you know the tiara Casey Roy loves and wears all the time? The one she got from Grandma Mabel? Yesterday, I borrowed it. I only wanted to wear it for a little bit, but then I went to go pee and I forgot I was wearing it and when I went to flush, the tiara fell into the toilet with my pee! Oh no!

I took it out (ew!) and washed it. I was going to confess, but then Casey Roy was mean to me again today. She told me I should put a bag over my head! Can you believe that, for crying out loud? I guess she's going to be wearing a pee-tiara after all!

All the best!

Sammy Roy!

The Oregon Trail

One Saturday afternoon, I accidentally set Sammy on fire. We were playing *Donner Party* and the three of us, huddled in our broken-down Conestoga wagon, were the only people left. I was starring in the role of the mother—resolute even in the face of certain doom. Casey and Sammy were playing supporting roles as my daughters (Clementine and Esmeralda). We had already eaten their brothers, Steve and Burt, as well as my husband, Brad.

The brutal winter night descended like a coffin lid and I swaddled Sammy and Casey against the bitter cold. I had wrapped Casey in a rough, woolen blanket and Sammy in The Quilt—the one we were never supposed to use for our games because it was very fragile and had been passed down through our family for generations. The thing was, it was the perfect blanket to use precisely *because* it was an antique heirloom that had been passed down through our family for generations. We might be forced to use saltines to simulate hardtack and make our tea with hot tap water, but here was something that could bring the whole scene to life!

And at that moment, Sammy looked like the most authentic blue mummy a set director could want. I lit the candle and used a few drops of the wax to affix it to a saucer from The Good China— something else we weren't supposed to touch. It's like our parents didn't even trust their own children sometimes.

I laid the candle on the rumpled blankets of my unmade bed and proceeded to stroke Sammy's feverish brow. This was my favorite part of the game. Casey and I both loved to sing, but neither of us liked to listen. However, since it fit into the plot, it was admissible. These times were rare and I took full advantage. I made up the song as I went along, drawing out the experience for as long as I could.❖

"Look Mother, it's morning!" Casey said, in a weak attempt to move the storyline forward.

"No, Clementine," I explained. "That's just the glow of the town burning. It won't be morning for hours yet. Just relax thyself and I'll sing you to sleep."

"I'm asleep already," she said impatiently.

"Then shut thyself up, Clementine."

Resuming my song, I soon became so enraptured I didn't realize what I'd done. Sometime during my exuberant gesticulation, I had knocked over the candle and the quilt was beginning to smolder.

"Alex!" Sammy yelled, wriggling in vain.

❖ This was key and both Casey and I were masters. Often, the bargain was "one song," so if you chose an actual song, there was a definite ending. On the other hand, if it was a song of your own composition, it could go on for hours. Without ever intending to, we had invented musical filibustering. And if that's not just as good as penicillin, I don't know what is.

"Hush little one," I soothed. "I won't let Clementine eat you. I'll keep you safe."

"Alex, look!" She tried to point but was too tightly bound.

"Shhh. You're delirious from the fever. Just be quiet and I'll sing you to sleep."

The flames were getting higher and now Casey noticed. She started laughing.

"Mother!" she hooted. "You're cooking Esmeralda!"

Dear Diary,

Emily Dickinson wrote, "Because I could not stop for death, he kindly stopped for me." Well, today death stopped for me and I said, "Nobody's home, sucker!"

Casey Roy says Alex Roy owes me BIG TIME because she set me on fire. I said it was fine because, first of all, I wasn't hurt and second of all, it was the most exciting thing that happened to me all morning! Casey Roy says Alex Roy owes her too, for not tattle-telling. She says Alex Roy is going to pay BIG TIME.

All the best!

Sammy Roy!

P.S. We agreed it was best to hide The Quilt. If Jillian Roy, my mom, saw it, she would be very sad and a little mad. Or maybe, she would be very mad and a little sad. Or MAYBE she would be very mad and very sad. I think it's not very likely that she would be only a little mad and a little sad—

especially if she also found out about The Good China.

P.P.S. Probably it's best if we take a break from playing Oregon Trail. Think about it. If it is this dangerous now, imagine how it was in REAL Olden Times!

Zoltron

Alex: still 12

Casey: still 10

Sammy: still 6

Roy's Regret: ageless and evergreen

Mom & Dad: old and they surely have to know it at this point

Aunt Hattie: The reason she was God's secretary is because first she was his mom and then after he moved out and got a job, she had nothing to do because nothing had been invented yet so she had to go work for him! Ha ha ha!

Sneaky Snoopers

It was only a matter of time before Casey and Sammy invented a game that didn't include me. It was called *Sneaky Snoopers* and, as the name would suggest, meant sneaking around the house and spying on people. They made fake walkie-talkies and annoyed everyone—most of all, me.

For the most part, *Sneaky Snoopers* operated out of Casey's bedroom (otherwise known as the most forbidden room in the house).[❖]

Once in a while they'd go on assignment.

"The subject is in the kitchen," I'd hear Sammy whisper from the other room. "The subject appears to be making a sandwich."

"Sammy, cut it out," I'd snap.

"The subject seems to be aggravated."

"Go in for a closer look," Casey would instruct from under the dining room table. "I'll cover you."

"Leave me alone," I'd say in a huff.

[❖] She would regularly put baby powder on the floor to detect the footprints of any unsuspecting invader. I can only imagine her plan was then to track them down and catch them white-footed, so to speak. That was never necessary because whenever you did go through her room, you were smart enough to do it quickly. I'm sure you can see where this is headed. So slipping on the baby powder and crashing to the floor would be more than enough to alert Casey. No need for gum-shoeing. The only consolation was that Casey was often so eager to nab the prey she'd caught in her web that she would dash into her own room. And you can probably figure out how that ended up.

"The subject is telling me to leave her alone."

"Mom!" I'd call.

"The subject is calling for her mommy."

"You're on your own," Casey would say, knowing what was coming.

"That's it, Sammy!" I'd screech, running after her.

"The subject is hostile! Repeat—the subject is hostile!" she'd yell as we'd race through the house.

The Grate

The reason Casey's room served as *Sneaky Snoopers* Headquarters was because of the grate. Her room was right above the kitchen and because the house was from Olden Times, her heat came from directly below. However, along with heat came conversations and, if you know anything about anything, you know the juiciest conversations happen in the kitchen. Normally, you wouldn't be able to understand more than the occasional word. But, if you got a screwdriver from Mom's toolbox, unscrewed the grate, pried off the cover and stuck your head inside, you could actually hear quite well.

And since Casey is so nosey, eavesdropping became one of her favorite hobbies. Furthermore, she didn't need to worry about anyone catching her since she made such great efforts to keep people out.❖

❖ This included a sign posted on the door that read, "Only knock in case of an emergency." Subsequently, my mom would get a great kick out of knocking on it every evening and saying calmly, "Casey. Time for dinner. It's an emergency."

Button-Licking

There was a reason we would risk our lives to go through Casey's room. Since our house was from Olden Times, there were two staircases. The first was normal and led directly to Casey's room. The second was at the other end of the house and it was so steep and narrow it might as well have been a ladder. That was the one the servants in Olden Times would use. It led to my room, which of course was a great source of amusement to Casey.

Sammy's room was next to Casey's. Multiple times a day, she faced a quandary. Should she walk the length of the house, go down the sketchy stairs, and walk the length of the house again, just to get to the kitchen or the front door? Or, should she simply nip down through Casey's room and— *voila!* Most times, she wouldn't risk the wrath, but occasionally, when she just wanted a quick snack, the convenience was just too tempting to resist.

One afternoon, while Casey and I were washing dishes, there was a huge crash above us. We looked up to see a leg coming through the ceiling. Apparently, while engaging in her new avocation, Casey had decided not to replace the grate in her room, which left a hole in the floor, perfect for ensnaring an unsuspecting trespasser.

When Sammy tried using her shortcut, she fell right through.

"Oh no!" I screamed. "Sammy, are you okay?"

"I don't know," she whimpered from above.

I looked at Casey, who was fuming into such a rage I thought she might turn green and triple in size.

"GET OUT OF MY ROOM!" Casey ran up the stairs with me right behind her.

The last thing I saw as I dashed out of the kitchen was Sammy's leg wriggling frantically as she tried to free herself before the maelstrom that was our sister descended. I reached Casey's bedroom a split-second after she did, which was a split-second after Sammy had extracted herself from the floor. Unfortunately, there was not even enough time for Sammy to get a reasonable head start, much less reach the safety of her own room. Casey was as fast a runner as she was a reader.

Instead, Sammy made the second of four very bad decisions. Rather than trying her luck at escaping or facing her foe, neither of which I admit had much chance of success, our Daniel went even deeper into the lion's den—Casey's closet.

Casey immediately lunged after her in an effort to tug the closet door open and I could hear Sammy's muffled cries from within.

"Casey, what are you doing?" I shouted, rushing over to push on the door.

Fear and adrenaline can lend a person considerable strength, but even so, Sammy's six-year-old muscles were not going to last long against the lioness defending her territory.

Then, in a flash decision that would impress even the most seasoned military general, Casey switched strategies. Instead of trying to open the door, she tried to do the opposite. And so with the combined force of the three of us pulling and pushing in the *same* direction, the door slammed shut with such force that the handle came loose.

"There!" Casey grunted, ripping off the doorknob and effectively locking Sammy in the closet for the foreseeable future. "That'll teach you to ever go in my room again!"

I'd seen this side of Casey. As she stood there, seething and breathing heavily, there was only one way of dealing with her—complete submission.

"She won't, Case," I assured in an even, subdued tone. "Right, Sammy?"

Here's something you should know about Sammy. She is quite easily the sweetest, most sympathetic and thoughtful person I've ever met. She loves and accepts everyone, just like a dog. However, she's also the most stubborn person I've ever met and, on the rare occasion someone does get her dander up, she has a fierce temper that makes her a formidable opponent. In fact, I would go so far as to say that if a mugger ever tried to take something from her that she wasn't willing to give up—I would fear *for* the mugger.

"Sammy?" I repeated.

That's when Sammy made her third very bad decision. She poked the lion.

Kicking the door furiously, she screamed, "Casey! I'm going to strangle you!"

Casey's hysteria grew exponentially. "Not if I don't let you out, you won't!"

"Sammy?" I tried again, racking my brain for some way to defuse the situation.

Sammy quieted as she considered her options. And it turns out, Casey isn't the only one who can switch strategies mid-stream. It was then Sammy made her fourth and final very bad decision.

"Casey?" Sammy said slyly.

"What?" Casey demanded in the haughty tones of the victor.

"Your clothes are in here," she said in a creepy, singsong voice.

The look of victory flew off Casey's face—replaced by one I can only describe as akin to the expression on the face of the Wicked Witch of the West after Dorothy threw the bucket of water on her. "Don't you dare touch my clothes!" Casey wailed.

"I'm touching your clothes, Casey," Sammy continued to sing in mock serenity.

"YOU BETTER STOP!"

"Mmm," Sammy crooned. "Now, I'm licking all the buttons."

Later, my parents came home and my dad removed the door from its hinges. Sammy was free and, within a few weeks, things were back to normal.

It was, however, the end of *Sneaky Snoopers*.

Ladyfingers

Not long afterward, my parents took all of us to Maine for a few weeks to visit Aunt Hattie. I think they may have also said something about an interview with some biological cemetery, but I'm not entirely sure about that part. What I *am* entirely sure of is The Ladyfingers.

You see, Aunt Hattie was a member of the D.A.R.✥ and she was hosting a tea party in her parlor. Aunt Hattie's parlor was absolutely off limits. It had exquisite furniture, which was really old and really expensive. It was definitely a room you wanted to avoid as a kid, especially if you had some markers with loose caps and even if your younger sister was annoying you and you just needed a little *space* for crying out loud!

But that's another story. In this story, the furniture is still immaculate and unmarred. So Aunt Hattie was having these D.A.R. broads over and somehow she hoodwinked us into helping with the whole brouhaha. She asked me to pour tea. She convinced both my mother and Sammy to wear

---

✥ D.A.R. stands for Daughters of the American Revolution, which means they were a bunch of old white ladies who thought they were better than everyone else. Casey and I called them the Dames Advocating Racism, because we were taught to call a fig, a fig. However, none of this is particularly pertinent to this story. For the purpose of this story, basically the guests were a bunch of people Aunt Hattie wanted desperately to impress.

dresses. She said something to Casey that made her agree to "watch her mouth and her attitude, thank you very much." Finally, she asked my mother to make Ladyfingers and Sammy to serve them.

In case you don't know, Ladyfingers are sponge cakes with an elongated, oval shape—kind of like fingers. Usually people put filling inside them, like cream or tiramisu or something like that. They are delicious and delicate and classy and most definitely high-brow, which was exactly the kind of food Aunt Hattie wanted to serve at her fancy-schmancy shindig. Believe me, there was no way Aunt Hattie was going to just bust out a box of *Oreos* and holler, "Have at 'em, girls!"

The afternoon came and the doors to the parlor were opened. Everything was as if in a dream. The setting was opulent. Casey's posture was perfect. I was gracious and grammatically correct. And according to the D.A.R., Sammy was "just the most cunnin'✢ little thing they ever did see." Even my mother was on her best behavior.

Then, as with many dreams, things took a turn. They went from lovely to confusing, from confusing to bizarre, from bizarre to horrifying and from horrifying to it's-a-wonder-Aunt-Hattie-still-speaks-to-us.

✢ This is Maine for "sweet, precious and charming."

D.A.R Catastrophe

You have to picture it in slow motion, because that's exactly how it happened—very cinematically. First, there were the "ladyfingers" themselves. True to her word, my mother had made them and they were certainly delicious. The tiny, oval cakes had a sweet, whipped filling and they were beautifully arranged atop a paper doily on a silver tray. What my mother did, however, was add her own signature flair. With a tube of bright red frosting, my mother "augmented" the cookies to make them look more realistic. She made the Ladyfingers actually look like *ladies'* fingers. And since my mother was not a woman to do anything by halves, she really went all out. There were polished nails and ruby rings and knuckles galore— all in great detail.

In the end, The Ladyfingers were horrific *and* tasty, all at the same time.

Now, here was the second part. As requested, Sammy served The Ladyfingers, traveling from one D.A.R. to the next. But she too added her own individual twist. Instead of just offering them with a smile, she said, "Would you like a Ladyfinger?" But after saying it so many times, the words became jumbled and soon turned to, "Lady, would you like me to give you the finger?"

And if that wasn't already about to give Aunt Hattie a heart attack, Sammy was saying all of these things in her—you guessed it—Satan Voice.

Dear Diary,

First of all, I cannot believe that I am the one grounded for all this when I didn't do a single thing. Seriously! Nothing. What went down today was none of my fault.

Okay, maybe a little bit, but how was I supposed to know Sammy was going to do that? She NEVER follows my instructions!

Imprisoned unjustly,

K.C. the Innocent

P.S. Frankly, what Mom did was sooo much worse, but nobody grounded HER!

P.P.S. Thank the Lord! Tonight we fly home and I won't have to choke on Aunt Hattie's condemnation and cigarettes anymore. The next time Mom and Dad try to bring me to Maine, I'm going to get myself thrown in jail.

Dear Diary,

Wow! When Aunt Hattie gets mad, she gets M-A-D! I don't know why Casey Roy thought it would be funny, because it sure wasn't. I'm not certain, but I think Aunt Hattie may have lost all of her nice friends. That's soooo sad! I told her that Kitty Kit and I would still be her friends, but I'm not sure if she heard me. She had just finished another Stinger and she may have been asleep.

If Aunt Hattie was M-A-D, then Alex Roy was livid! That's a new word I learned from when Alex Roy told Casey Roy, "I'm livid!" Then Alex Roy said, "I wish that kidnapper HAD taken you!" What's going on with my family? I'm so confused.

All the best!
Sammy Roy!

Dear Diary,

My heart is breaking. Every time I try to get back my good sister Alex, I mess things up. I want life to be like it used to be, but she only sees the bad in me. I know there is bad, but there is also so much good.

When she protected me and saved my life from that kidnapper, I knew she cared about me as much as I cared about her. Today, when she said she regretted it, my soul was crushed to a million pieces. The splotches on this page are my tears.

I've decided to try one more time to get her to see the real me, her adoring sister. Maybe then she will take back what she said, even if she does wish she hadn't saved me from the clutches of evil.

With a tiny sparkle of hope,
K.C. the Desolate

Dear Alix,

At times I feel alone and without light. But those moments are very few because of your love and friendship. That is my beacon.

I can't imagine life without you. I love you so. And I'm sorry for the times I've hurt you, because I regret them more than I can say, but I'm not perfect. I wish I could be the perfect sister because that's what you deserve, and instead you were stuck with one big disappointment. But this disappointment wants you to know she loves you.

I love you so very much.

K.C. the Disappointment

Frisky & the Flower
by Sammy Roy!

Once upon a time there was a girl named Julie. She had a cat and his name was Frisky. Julie had a mom and a step-dad. One day, she planted a flower and the flower was a Dandelion.

Then her mother died. She was very sad but it was true and she had to get on with her life. Julie and Frisky went into the woods and cried for a long time. She decided to go home. Julie didn't see that her tears were gone. In fact, Frisky told little ants and caterpillars to take them. They had put them on the flower. Every day Julie and Frisky went to cry by the flower.

Today was Thursday. Frisky took Julie to see the flower and it was large and beautiful.

The End

Sammy: please deliver this to Casey, who is probably sulking in her room. I hate to involve you in our dispute, but I'm sure you can understand the situation has deteriorated that much.

P.S. I enjoyed your story about Frisky and the Flower. I'm glad you've found a way to develop yourself as we undergo these tribulations.

Dear Casey,

My advice to you is to spend less time writing me letters and more time asking for Aunt Hattie's forgiveness. You wronged her, Casey. You wronged her BIG TIME!

Sincerely,

A. Roy

P.S. If you feel alone and without light, maybe you should try leaving your room for once and buy yourself a lamp.

Sammy: deliver this to Alix. She lives in her bedroom, which is on the corner of Sanctimonious Street and Bossy Boulevard.

Dear Alix,

    I don't know how you got an "A" in spelling. It's K.C.! Maybe it's time you started honoring a little thing I like to call Personal Expression. That's why I'm calling you "Alix." It's for your own good. You're living under the Roy Regime and you do everything the dictators say—even how to spell your own name!

    Your sister,

    K.C. the Revolutionary

P.S. It'll be a cold day in hell before I ever ask for Aunt Hattie's forgiveness. She's positively diabolical and I did her a favor.

Sammy: please deliver this to Casey, who is probably in her room making a bunch of political propaganda.

Dear "K.C.,"

The entire planet took a vote this morning and it was unanimous. Everyone thinks you need to get over yourself.

Sincerely,
A. Roy

P.S. Did you notice I honored your "personal expression"? That's because I'm a person of high moral caliber.

Dear Casey Roy and Alex Roy,

I am sad because my two favorite sisters are mad at each other. Jillian Roy says you're giving each other the cold shoulder, but she's wrong. It's the cold elbow and eyeball too! That's so mean. I want you to love each other as much as I love you. Then I will be happy! I'll be happy for two reasons. First, it'll be nice to have you back showing your love by fighting out loud. Second, I'm getting tired of delivering your letters back and forth. Plus, it's boring! It almost makes me want to play Oregon Trail again. Yikes!

I am also sad because of what Walt Roy calls Poor Time Management. That means these shenanigans (that's what he is calling you downstairs, just so you know) are wasting time we could be using to play an adventure. You two shenanigans are also doing Poor Time Management because I've been keeping track and so far this letter has taken me an hour to type.

In conclusion, I am sad and tired and bored. Please love each other again. I'm sick of you two shenanigans and I want my sisters back.

All the best!

Sammy Roy!

P.S. I almost forgot to tell you that even though I'm sad, I sure have been learning a lot of new words. You may have made me tired, but you also made me smarter! Here are the top ones:

1. Sanctimonious: hallway.
2. Deteriorated: not being able to walk across the sanctimonious.
3. Hell: where Casey would apologize to Aunt Hattie in the winter.
4. Shenanigans: sisters.
5. Regime: roof.
6. Diabolical: old and funny.
7. Dictators: Mom and Dad.
8. Sulking: reading inappropriate books.
9. Political Propaganda: clothes for Fatty Catty.

Dear Sammy,

You're one to talk! I hear you with that typewriter, click-clacking away all morning. It sounds like nails in the coffin of my childhood!

Abysmally,

K.C. the Buried Alive

P.S. You're not half as smart as you think. Maybe instead of wasting your time on that stupid typewriter, you should get a job and earn some money to buy a dictionary!

P.P.S. To Alex (because I know you read other people's mail), using quotes around my name is juvenile, petty, stupid, dumb and stupid!

P.P.P.S. And if Sammy tells Mom and Dad I said hell, I'm going to throw her stupid typewriter out the window!

Dear K.C.,
Here's a poem to express my feelings:

There once was a sister named K.C.
And everyone thought she was spacey.
We tried hard to find,
One time she'd been kind
But only found times she was lazy!

If you don't understand this poem, it's about how important is it to be nice, especially to your sisters. Sammy is crying in my room right now and I can't comfort her because I'm too busy writing you poems to try to make you understand what a selfish and inconsiderate person you are.
Sincerely,
A. Roy

P.S. Did you see how I wrote your "name"? That's called acquiescence.

P.P.S. In case you don't know what "acquiescence" means, it means peace offering. It's something humble people do that shows they are better than everyone else. And that's not mean because it's true.

Dear Alex,

You're one to talk!

Ostracized,

K.C. the Indignant

P.S. I wrote a few poems about you too, but they are all too deep for your puny brain to understand. Also, you are so mean to me it makes me cry too, but I have too much class to do it in front of other people.

P.P.S. If Sammy is crying because I called her stupid, you can tell her I'm sorry and it's not her fault. If she's crying over her stupid typewriter you can tell her to get a grip.

P.P.P.S. Of course I know what acquiescence means, dumbo. Do you know what a truce is? I'm bored.

Dear Alex, K.C. and Sammy,*

I never thought I'd say this, but it's too quiet around here. I understand there are many hurt feelings and I know it is hard to forgive one another. Be assured, your mother and I forgive you and God will always forgive you no matter what happens. Aunt Hattie may take a little longer, but she'll come around.

When you are older, you will look back on this time and see how precious it was. You will wish you had spent more time cherishing it and each other. In the Gospel according to Matthew (Chapter 22, Verse 39), God tells us to love our neighbor as ourselves. I'm confident that if you set aside your differences and reconcile with one another, you will all be happier.

I love you and I am so proud of each of you,
Dad

_____

* This is Dad's letter about how Aunt Hattie isn't as good as God, which we certainly didn't *him* to tell us, for crying out loud.

Dear Alex, K·C· and Sammy,

Did you notice I'm writing this on the back of a recycled envelope? There's a reason for that. You goils are wasting a lot of paper up there. It's time to cowgirl up. I can't imagine playing "Soap Opera" is nearly as much fun as taking down curtains and rearranging the furniture down here.

Love,

JR

Dear GREAT Aunt Hattie,

Walt and I have some shocking news for you. We've decided to become ministers. No, that's not the shocking news. We're moving to Maine. No, that's not the shocking news either. All of the girls are getting along! You'd have to see it to believe it and I hope you'll come see us soon.

Love,

JR

Dear Aunt Hattie, *

I was just settling down with a cup of coffee and a little Vivaldi to write you a letter about some exciting changes in our lives. Then Jillian told me she already "took care of it." I can only imagine what that means. Suffice it to say, Jillian and I have long felt called to be ministers of the gospel and to serve God in a new way. Now, we have answered that call. In one sense, this entails many logistical changes. We're selling the house here in Seattle and moving to Maine, where we'll begin studying at

---

* Basically, this letter is giving Aunt Hattie fair warning in case she wants to move out of Maine. There's also some business about being on two "journeys," but I haven't the faintest clue what that's all about. Last time I checked, you can only have one at a time. Casey says it's supposed to be "metaphysical," but I'm pretty sure that's not even a word. I'd ask Dad, who knows every word on the planet and has an hour-long etymological lesson prepared on each one just in case, but then I'd have to admit I've been reading his mail and I would *so* get sent to my room for that. By the way, I'm not sure if "etymological" is a word either, but it's a heck of a lot more likely to be one than "metaphysical," which sounds like a new-age facial treatment if you ask me.

Bangor Theological Seminary in September. In another sense, we are embarking on a spiritual journey to lands unknown, full of fear and promise.

We're not sure where we'll be living, but we very much hope you will share our home. It would be wonderful to have you around and you yourself are quick to remind us what a positive influence you are on the girls.

Anyway, something to think about. I'll write more as we know more.

Much love and God bless,

Walt

Dear Walter and Jillian,

Call me certifiably insane, but I would like you and the girls to live here with me. I don't imagine I have too many years left, but if I do, I might as well waste them on this as anything. Besides, I sure do miss Alex's cooking.

Perhaps you'll become MY "Roy's Regret." Ha ha ha. I do have a few requests.

1. I have my schedule and you all can work around it.
2. I'd like fish on Fridays.
3. No Satan Voice.
4. If one hair of Kitty Kit's is shaved, the deal is off.

Aunt Hattie

Dear Aunt Hattie, *

Tonight, Jillian and I told the girls the big news. Some of them took it better than others. I suppose that was to be expected. It will certainly be an adjustment for all of us.

We haven't told them about living with you yet. Jillian thought it best to dole out the news a little at a time, especially for Casey who struggles so with change. I think putting her in the room with the books and getting her a library card upon arrival will help ease the transition considerably.

I suppose I should get back to packing.
Much love and God bless,
Walt

---

* Basically, this says they haven't told Casey we'll be moving in with Aunt Hattie, which is smart since she's going to go ballistic when she finds out. It also says they plan to give Casey The Boys' Room, which totally isn't fair.

Dear Diary,

Today, Mom told us over dinner she has decided to become a minister. Casey said, "Oh blank," and got sent to her room. It wasn't actually a "blank" if you know what I mean.

After dinner, Mom was cleaning up in the kitchen and Dad told us he had decided to become a minister too. Casey (who had been let out of her room by this point) called him a copycat and got sent back to her room. I asked him if he had told Mom yet and if she said whether or not it was okay. I didn't get sent to my room, but he did give me a very, very stern look. I'll have to ask Aunt Hattie about that.

I've thought about this a long time and I'm pretty sure I'm going to need another notebook. I've already filled up this one and nothing really interesting has even happened yet!

Sincerely,
A. Roy

Dear Diary,

Hooray! Mom and Dad are going back to school to become ministers and we're moving to Maine! I'm so excited! And even more great news. We're going to live with Aunt Hattie! Casey Roy isn't going to like that one bit! I will though! Aunt Hattie is so so so funny for crying out loud!

Sometimes I think my life can't get any betterer!

All the best!

Sammy Roy!

Dear Diary,

Crap! Mom and Dad are going back to school to become ministers and we're moving to Maine! Why does everything bad have to happen to ME? I'm devastated!!!! Now we have to believe in God ALL THE TIME! More horrific news: we'll be living in the same town as Aunt Hattie. Can my life get any worse?

Miserable and homeless,

K.C. the Transplanted

P.S. If someone is reading this, now you know why I look so sorrowful.

P.P.S. It could be worse. We could have to LIVE with Aunt Hattie!

The Legacy

Scene opens with Jillian and Alex sitting on a pile of boxes in the front yard, waiting for Walt to arrive with the moving truck. They are wearing matching overalls, which Jillian bought for all five family members, and red bandanas to keep their hair back as they work. Alex's hair now touches her shoulders.

Jillian *(in an exceedingly rare moment of reflection, considering she is usually all action-action-action):* Alex, you should have your own planet.

Alex: Huh?

Jillian: Pay attention, Alex.

Alex *(affronted)*: I am paying attention. What do you mean, my own planet?

Jillian: Like Arvon is for me.

Alex *(starting to sound nervous):* What do you mean, "like Arvon is for you?"

Jillian *(sighs)*: Alex, if you're not going to use the smart part of your brain, I'm not going to give you advice. And you and your sisters are forever pestering me to tell you how to run your own lives.

I never met people who wanted to be told what to do as much as you three *goils*.

Alex *(after a considerable pause)*: So what you are telling me is that Arvon isn't a real place.

Jillian *(ponders a moment)*: Let's just say it's a place you can only visit in here *(she taps her head)* and in here (*she taps her heart).*

Alex *(her head reeling since her entire world view has just been completely knocked off its axis)*: Okay.

Jillian *(either oblivious or indifferent to the response of her daughter to this bombshell)*: It won't be long now before you'll be out of the nest and navigating through what some people call the "real world."

Alex *(aghast and incredulous)*: Mom, I'm 12!

Horn honks as Walt pulls up in front of the house.

Jillian (*stands up and pats Alex on the back):* You're welcome, toots.

Zoltron

Zoltron is my planet. I don't know a whole lot about it yet. Truth be told, I'm still adjusting to the idea that I even *have* a planet. So I'm not sure about topography and weather patterns and all that jazz. And I certainly don't know about the people and whatever their cultures and traditions are. In fact, pretty much all I have is the name.

And why am I calling it Zoltron? Just on the off-chance that imaginary planets are organized alphabetically. Lord knows, I love my mother unconditionally and multiversally, but I think we can all agree a girl needs some breathing room—especially when her parents have just turned her entire world upside down and inside out.

I think I'll try orbiting around myself for a while.

About the Author

Robin Russell lives in Seattle and teaches writing to middle-school students. She is half-Arvonian and the oldest of three sisters. For more information, visit www.robinrussell.net.

Character Fonts

Aunt Hattie: Lucinda Sans Typewriter, Rage Italic
Walt Roy: Freestyle Script
Jillian Roy: MV Boli
Alex Roy: Kristen ITC
Casey Roy: Ugly Rumor*(Ace Fonts)
Sammy Roy: Wishing on a Star (Des Gomez), Lucinda Sans Typewriter, Ice Cream Sandwich (Des Gomez)
Roy's Regret: He's a dog, duh. Of course it's Times New Roman.

---

* No, for real. That's what it's called.

Summer 1971

Dear Aunt Harriet,

Thank you for your nice, easy-to-read letter. Thank you also for opening up a bank account for Robin so far away. This way she is sure to see all of it at the proper time.

Sounds as if you and Peter are having a memorable summer. It's refreshing to hear of someone treating a 12-year-old person as an adult rather than as a child. Do you think Ed and Lynn will ever let another one of theirs visit with you for such a long time? When we feel it's time for Robin to learn the ways of the world we will send her to you.

If you would like some good inspiration for making a fist, you will have to come out here and watch Robin. She does it quite well. We are getting some pictures taken this week and will send you one as soon as we receive them. You did get the one of her at six hours, didn't you? Keep up the exercises and don't throw out any old children's books.

Thank you again, much love,
Jennifer